SATURDAY LUNCH
WITH THE
BROWNINGS

SATURDAY LUNCH WITH THE BROWNINGS

PENELOPE MORTIMER

WITH AN INTRODUCTION BY LUCY SCHOLES

DAUNT BOOKS

This edition first published in
the United Kingdom in 2020 by
Daunt Books
83 Marylebone High Street
London W1U 4QW

I

Copyright © Penelope Mortimer 1960
Introduction copyright © Lucy Scholes 2020

First published by Hutchinson 1960

Many of the stories in this collection were
first published in *The New Yorker*

Sections of the introduction appeared originally
in slightly different forms on *The Paris Review
Daily* (2019) and *NYR Daily* (2018)

The right of Penelope Mortimer to be identified as
Proprietor of this work has been asserted by her in accor-
dance with the Copyright, Designs and Patents Act 1988.

A CIP catalogue record for this title
is available from the British Library.

ISBN 978-1-911547-72-3

Typeset by Marsha Swan
Printed and bound by TJ International Ltd,
Padstow, Cornwall

www.dauntbookspublishing.co.uk

CONTENTS

ACKNOWLEDGEMENTS

My thanks are due to the editor of *The New Yorker*, in whose columns the majority of these stories first appeared.

P. M.

PUBLISHERS' NOTE

This book was originally published in 1960. It is a historical text and for this reason we have not made any changes to its use of language.

INTRODUCTION

During the late 1950s, when she wrote the twelve superb stories included in *Saturday Lunch with the Brownings* (the majority of which first appeared in *The New Yorker*), Penelope Mortimer was famous for being the beautiful, lauded authoress wife of the renowned barrister-cum-writer, John Mortimer. Profiles of the couple featured in magazines ranging from *Good Housekeeping* to *Tatler*, often accompanied by photographs with their picture-perfect six children. Wife and mother were the identities that defined Mortimer, even as a writer. She had a regular parenting column, 'Five Girls and a Boy', in the *Evening Standard*, and her fiction, both her short stories and the four novels she'd published thus far – *Johanna* (1947; under the name Penelope Dimont, as she was then); *A Villa in*

Summer (1954); *The Bright Prison* (1956); and *Daddy's Gone A-Hunting* (1958) – dealt predominantly with the subjects of marriage and motherhood.

She wasn't writing twee, cosy tales of domestic bliss though; instead Mortimer penned sharp, shrewd portraits of marital infidelity, strained, unhappy housewives and their insensitive husbands, impotently railing against the draining demands of parenthood, more often than not drowning their sorrows in drink. Much of this material she drew from her own life, especially when it came to her short stories, for which there was 'no need to look for ideas', as she put it in *About Time Too* (1993), her second volume of memoirs: 'I mined my life for incidents with a beginning, a middle and an end, finding even the dreariest of days contained nuggets of irony, farce, unpredictable behaviour.' The cracks in her and John's marriage, and the conflicts associated with finding much of her worth and value in her role of caregiver, while at the same time feeling stifled by domesticity, all provided rich fodder for her fiction. *Daddy's Gone A-Hunting*, for example, the book that precedes *Saturday Lunch with the Brownings*, depicts a suburban mother's attempts to procure an abortion for her student daughter (a situation Mortimer had recently found herself in when her eldest daughter, then at university, fell pregnant). It was a daring topic for its day, as evidenced by the resistance and disgust with which Mortimer's protagonist Ruth's attempts are met: 'You would really advise her to do this thing? Your own daughter? Good God Ruth, I'm sorry. You make me sick,' expostulates the family GP when she turns to him for help. The reviews, however, were excellent. 'A remarkable and deeply disturbing achievement,' declared one.

Mortimer – who, by the time she died, at the age of 81 in 1999, had published nine novels, this one story collection, two volumes of memoir, a biography of the Queen Mother, screenplays, and an abundant body of journalism – drew more heavily on her lived experience than most, not least because it proved such a reliable source of creative stimulus. Family life is her subject, and in *Saturday Lunch with the Brownings*, which was first published in 1960, she picks it apart with precise, swift, agile strokes. 'No one knows better how to catalogue in easy narrative the minutiae of domestic life,' admitted one critic admiringly when the collection was first published, 'or how to undermine domestic life's apparent security.' Mortimer has a keen eye for the horror underneath the banality of the everyday, in particular that moment when someone familiar and benign turns monstrous.

In 'Little Mrs Perkins', for example, a seemingly sweet, vulnerable, young mother-to-be is ensconced in the bed next to the narrator, who is in a nursing home recovering from the birth of her third child. The roommates don't speak across the curtain that separates them – 'a fixed, insurmountable barrier dividing our two lives' – but the bored narrator watches and listens, first with sympathy, then with morbid fascination and shock as Mrs Perkins is put on strict bed rest and told she won't be able to take the forthcoming trip to Tenerife that she and her husband have scheduled:

> slowly, cautiously, she was pushing back the blankets with her feet [...] Then, very carefully, she raised one leg into the air; its shadow through the curtain was long, thin, wavering. She bent her knee, pushed the leg straight again. Afterwards, still very slowly and carefully, the other leg. She was testing something – but what? One leg. Then the other leg. No noise, no unusual creaking of the bedsprings. Both legs circling, faster and faster. She was trying not to make a noise. She was bicycling.

Despite being 'appalled' by what she's witnessing, the ineffective narrator watches the antics of the other woman in horrified silence. 'I did, I said, nothing,' she shamefully confesses.

Powerless protagonists appear regularly throughout the collection. In 'The White Rabbit', an eleven-year-old child is given a bunny by her estranged father, but is so disgusted by what the pet stands for – a rift in the intimacy between herself, her mother and her stepfather – that she creeps out of bed during the night and drops the creature over the balcony of their tenth-floor London apartment onto the busy road below. Both here and in 'The King of Kissingdom' – a warped fairy tale of a family romance about the neuroses of a guilt-ridden child of divorced parents – Mortimer demonstrates the keenest understanding of the interior world of childhood. Find a better sketch of sibling rivalry, for example, than that given by the narrator, who, looking back on her relationship with her elder brother, describes him as 'an impression of grey-flannel violence, a pair of stocky knees, a whiplash decapitating nettles'. Mortimer's empathetic, expert grasp of the child's perspective has often been overlooked, the emphasis put instead on her adult protagonists and the tantalising insights they offer into her own very public marriage.

Regardless of whether she's writing from the point of view of a child or that of an adult, she continually depicts family life as a fraught battleground. In the story from which the collection takes its title, husband and wife Madge and William Browning find themselves at each other's throats, arguing about their children (their youngest, Bessie, and her half-siblings: William's stepdaughters, Melissa and Rachel). It's a domestic scene permeated with violence; from the 'holocaust of cornflakes and burnt toast' amongst which the children breakfast, to the vehemence of William's outburst after Madge furiously berates him for striking Melissa: 'You think I'd stay with you and these delinquent little bitches of yours?' he screams at her. 'Get their father to keep them. Go on, go and find him. Tell him to keep the lot of you on his five pounds a week.'

When she and John met in 1948, Mortimer was already the mother of three daughters and pregnant with her fourth (the oldest two were fathered by her first husband, Charles Dimont, whom she married in 1937, when she was 19, and divorced twelve years later; her third by Kenneth Harrison; and her fourth by Randall Swingler). She and John then had two children together, another daughter and a son. In 'Saturday Lunch with the Brownings' – based on a very real argument in the Mortimer household, as Valerie Grove confirms in her biography *A Voyage Round John Mortimer* (2007) – William dotes on Bessie, 'his darling', but is short-tempered with her half-sisters. Yet even at his most unpleasant, William is more than just the one-dimensional villain of the piece. Mortimer takes pains to acknowledge how the demands of family life make victims of them all: called upon to referee Rachel and Bessie's breakfast-table squabbles, William is left feeling 'foolish and unhappy. Why did his days have to begin like this? What had he done to deserve it? What the hell was it all for?' As Grove perspicaciously notes, 'Penelope did more than milk their domestic life; her stories reflect how deeply and sympathetically she understood her children and how she also felt a fundamental empathy with her beleaguered, over-burdened husband.'

So too 'Such a Super Evening' gives readers a sneak peek behind the facade the Mortimers put on for their adoring public. In it, the Mathiesons – both 'fantastically successful writers' and the parents of eight children – are invited to dinner by a self-effacing housewife. Over the course of the evening their hostess is astonished to discover that the supposedly golden couple are actually bickering bores. Mortimer's fictionalisation of her own life allowed for some dramatic licence, but the underlying principal stands: her and John's marriage was not as perfect as it looked. Mortimer was struggling with depression – she took an overdose in 1956, and would do so again in 1962. She was worn ragged by motherhood and domesticity, writing in fits and starts between bouts of excruciating writer's block, her miserableness exacerbated by John's thoughtless infidelities. So much of Mortimer's identity was caught up in maternity and motherhood, but like many women of the era, she felt trapped in her role.

Nowhere are these contradictions more powerfully and cleverly explored here than in the opening story, 'The Skylight'. A masterclass in tension, it sees an unnamed mother and her five-year-old son arriving alone at their rented holiday home in the French countryside only to find the house locked and unassailable by any route other than a tiny open window in the roof. Despite the heat – which 'sank with the resonant hum of failing consciousness' – the story is steeped in dread from the start. The house is 'grey' and 'mean', its shutters and doors all 'heavy black timber' locked shut with 'iron bars', surrounded by 'dead grass' through which slinks a rat the size of a cat. Worn out by their journey and unable to think what else to do, the woman climbs up to the roof and lowers her son through the skylight into the attic, giving him strict instructions to make his way downstairs and unbolt a window – but the little boy disappears into the gloom. When mother and son are eventually reunited, her relief is tempered by frustration and rage at the distress he's caused her: 'With one hand she pushed him upright. With the other, she hit him. She struck him so hard that her palm stung.' Mortimer would later realise that this story was actually about a miscarriage she'd suffered shortly before writing it in 1959.

Two years later, in February 1961, Mortimer found herself pregnant again. At first she was excited. This was in large part due to the rather lukewarm reviews *Saturday Lunch with the Brownings* had received when it had been published the previous year. One especially hostile critic in the *Sunday Times* declared her unhappy couples 'trivially embittered, chronically quarrelling about nothing, filled with a fatigued desperation', and suggested they should just take fifty aspirin and end it all. Mortimer thought that a new baby might bring her the contentment the book hadn't. Instead, however, she had a termination – and a permanent sterilisation – at the encouragement of both her doctor (on medical grounds – she was 42) and John (who argued that their marriage, which was struggling, should come first). Devastatingly, while she was still in hospital recovering from the surgery, Mortimer discovered that John was having yet another affair, this time with the actor Wendy Craig, who shortly thereafter became pregnant by him.

Anyone who's read *The Pumpkin Eater* (1962), the work for which Mortimer remains most well known today, will be familiar with these events. When, after months of depression, Mortimer began writing again that November, she poured every last drop of her anguished experience into the novel, the story of a middle-class housewife's break-down following the collapse of her marriage. The result is raw, vivid and utterly magnificent. 'Almost every woman I can think of will want to read this book,' raved Edna O'Brien on its publication, and it was quickly adapted into a film (the screenplay was written by Harold Pinter, and Anne Bancroft was nominated for an Academy Award for Best Actress for her portrayal of the lead). Although much deserved, *The Pumpkin Eater*'s success immediately over-shadowed the comparatively meagre attention given to *Saturday Lunch with the Brownings*. Indeed, the collection undoubtedly suffered for having been published between Mortimer's two strongest works; it didn't quite live up to the obvious audaciousness of *Daddy's Gone A-Hunting*, then it was swamped by the formidable success of *The Pumpkin Eater*.

But more broadly, Mortimer's story is that of the struggle of survival. While critics were lauding *The Pumpkin Eater* as a masterpiece, Mortimer was recovering from the overdose she'd taken shortly before the novel's publication, and her subsequent hospitalisation for ECT treatment. Had this attempt on her life been successful, *The Pumpkin Eater* would have been one hell of a suicide note, destined to have been read alongside the likes of Sylvia Plath's *Ariel* (1965) and Hannah Gavron's *The Captive Wife: Conflicts of Housebound Mothers* (1966). Gavron, a comfortably middle-class, intelligent working wife and mother like Mortimer, took her own life in a Primrose Hill flat in 1965, in eerily similar circumstances to Plath, two years earlier, just one street away. Today, Plath and Gavron are both widely regarded as casualties of a particular time, on the cusp of second-wave feminism. Plath especially has been canonised as a feminist saint lost in battle. Mortimer's is a different story: she's the woman who didn't die, who got the divorce, went through the menopause and lived on, alone, into old age, her fame slowly and steadily diminishing. In short, she survived but her career and subsequent reputation didn't. Had Plath or Gavron also lived, one can't help but wonder whether they too would have suffered fates similar to Mortimer. Instead, death has embalmed them as figures of tragically untapped potential.

Mortimer and John divorced in 1971, when she was 53. But reinventing herself – both as far as she was concerned and in the eyes of others – proved an all but impossible task, however hard she tried. Her four final novels – *My Friend Says It's Bullet-Proof* (1967), *The Home* (1971), *Long*

Distance (1974), and *The Handyman* (1983) – are each candid explorations of middle-aged women starting over, whether after illness (mental and/or physical), divorce or widowhood. The most daring is *Long Distance*, a fragmentary and hallucinatory account of an unnamed woman's desperate journey through an unspecified institution – part rural artists' retreat, part hospital – that clearly draws on Mortimer's experiences of being hospitalised for depression. Her narrator is 'a blank slate, an empty glass', someone who's doomed to 'repeat experience until it is remembered'. It's Mortimer's boldest bid to rehabilitate herself, both as a woman and as a writer. As the critic Ronald Blyth noted, 'The sexual and spiritual progress of female middle age has rarely received such an excitingly imaginative treatment.' Yet despite such praise, and the fact that it was published in *The New Yorker* in its entirety – something the magazine hadn't done since J.D. Salinger's *Raise High the Roof Beam, Carpenters*, in 1955 – the novel failed to have the wider impact Mortimer hoped for. The figure of the broken housewife was clearly one the public could rally around, but that of the middle-aged divorcee battling her demons in order to secure for herself a fresh start apparently less so.

Although *The Pumpkin Eater* had resonated so poignantly with O'Brien, the Irish writer was twelve years younger than Mortimer, and that age gap, slight as it was, made all the difference. O'Brien's debut, *The Country Girls* (1960), kicked off the decade that brought us the sexual revolution and women's liberation. The invention of the Pill offered women reproductive choices previously unheard of, but so too the new narratives about motherhood that were being written by a younger generation of women – *The L-Shaped Room* (1960) by Lynne Reid Banks, for example, or Margaret Drabble's *The Millstone* (1965) or *The Waterfall* (1969) – bore little resemblance to those Mortimer had been writing.

The world in which Mortimer wrote her first novels had been a very different place: as a consequence, she found herself trying to fight her way out of the sexual stereotypes of the 1950s long after she'd left those years behind. This, combined with her lifelong inability to escape from the shadow of her and John's very public marriage, sealed her fate. Following her divorce Mortimer spent a lot of time in America, including two residencies at Yaddo (during the first she wrote *Long Distance*, and during the second, her first memoir, *About Time: An Aspect of Autobiography* (1979), which went on to win the prestigious Whitbread Prize), and stints teaching at The New School in New York and at Boston University. She also made a host of interesting friends, including Kurt Vonnegut, Edmund White, and Bette Davis. Yet despite these many achievements, she continued to be stalked by depression, along with a gnawing sense that she hadn't achieved what she should have in terms of her writing. She felt stifled by the woman she'd once been. When she died in 1999, sadly the legacy that remained was the same one she'd spent the previous four decades trying to escape. As she wrote in *About Time Too*, which was published only six years before her death: 'The outside world identified me as "ex-wife of John Mortimer, mother of six, author of *The Pumpkin Eater*" – accurate as far as it went, but to me unrecognisable.' With this in mind, reading *Saturday Lunch with the Brownings* is a bittersweet experience. On the one hand, it takes us back to a time before this identity had been foisted on her; but on the other, these excellent stories show a writer already wrestling with the issues that would continue to plague her for years to come.

Lucy Scholes, 2020

THE SKYLIGHT

The heat, as the taxi spiralled the narrow hill bends, became more violent. The road thundered between patches of shade thrown by overhanging rock. Behind the considerable noise of the car, the petulant hooting at each corner, the steady tick-tick of the cicadas spread through the woods and olive groves as though to announce their coming.

The woman sat so still in the back of the taxi that at corners her whole body swayed, rigid as a bottle in a jolting bucket, and sometimes fell against the five-year-old boy who curled, thumb plugged in his mouth, on the seat beside her. The woman felt herself disintegrate from heat. Her hair, tallow blonde, crept on her wet scalp. Her face ran off the bone like water off a rock – the bridges of nose, jaw and cheekbones must be drained of flesh by now. Her body poured away inside the too-tight cotton suit and only her bloodshot feet, almost purple in the torturing sandals, had any kind of substance.

'When are we there?' the boy asked.

'Soon.'

'In a minute will we be there?'

'Yes.'

A long pause. What shall we find, the mother asked herself. She wished, almost at the point of tears, that there were someone else to ask, and answer, this question.

'Are we at France now?'

For the sixth time since the plane had landed she answered, 'Yes, Johnny.'

The child's eyes, heavy-lidded, long-lashed, closed; the thumb stoppered his drooping mouth. Oh, no, she thought, don't let him, he mustn't go to sleep.

'Look. Look at the . . .' Invention failed her. They passed a shack in a stony clearing. 'Look at the chickens,' she said, pulling at the clamped stuff of her jacket. 'French chickens,' she added, long after they had gone by. She stared dully at the taxi driver's back, the dark stain of sweat between his shoulder blades. He was not the French taxi driver she had expected. He was old and quiet and burly, driving his cab with care. The price he had quoted for his forty kilometre drive from the airport had horrified her. She had to translate all distances into miles and then apply them, a lumbering calculation, to England.

How much, she had wanted to ask, would an English taxi driver charge to take us from London Airport to . . .? It was absurd. There was no one to tell her anything. Only the child asking his interminable questions, with faith.

'Where?' he demanded suddenly, sitting up.

She felt herself becoming desperate. It's too much for me, she thought. I can't face it. 'What do you mean – where?'

'The chickens.'

'Oh. They've gone. Perhaps there'll be some more, later on.'

'But when are we there?'

'Oh, *Jonathan* . . .' In her exasperation, she used his full name. He turned his head away, devouring his thumb, looking closely at the dusty rexine. When her hot, stiff body fell against him, he did not move. She tried to compose herself, to resume command.

It had seemed so sensible, so economical, to take this house for the summer. We all know, she had said (although she herself did not), what the French are – cheat you at every turn. And then, the horror of those Riviera beaches. We've found this charming little farmhouse up in the mountains – well, they say you can nip down to Golfe-Juan in ten minutes. In the car, of course. Philip will be driving the girls, but I shall take Johnny by air. I couldn't face those dreadful hotels with him. Expensive? But, my dear, you don't *know* what it cost us in Bournemouth last year, and I feel one owes them the sun. And then there's this dear old

3

couple, the Gachets, thrown in so to speak. They'll have it all ready for us, otherwise of course I couldn't face arriving there alone with Johnny. As it is, we shall be nicely settled when Philip and the girls arrive. I envy us too. I couldn't face the prospect of those awful public meals with Johnny – no, I just couldn't face it.

And so on. It was a story she had made up in the cold, well-ordered English spring. She could hear herself telling it. Now it was real. She was inadequate. She was in pain from the heat, and not a little afraid. The child depended on her. I can't face it, she thought, anticipating the arrival at the strange house, the couple, the necessity of speaking French, the task of getting the child bathed and fed and asleep. Will there be hot water, mosquitoes, do they know how to boil an egg? Her head beat with worry. She looked wildly from side to side of the taxi, searching for some sign of life. The woods had ended, and there was now no relief from the sun. An ugly pink house with green shutters stood away from the road; it looked solid, like an enormous brick, in its plot of small vines. Can that be it? But the taxi drove on.

'I suppose he knows where he's going,' she said.

The child turned on his back, as though in bed, straddling his thin legs. Over the bunched hand his eyes regarded her darkly, unblinking.

'Do sit *up*,' she said. His eyelids drooped again. His legs, his feet in their white socks and disproportionately large brown sandals, hung limp. His head fell to one side. 'Poor baby,' she said softly. 'Tired baby.' She managed to put an arm round him. They sat close, in extreme discomfort.

Suddenly, without warning, the driver swung the taxi off the road. The woman fell on top of the child, who struggled for a moment before managing to free himself. He sat up, alert, while his mother pulled and pushed, trying to regain her balance. A narrow, stony track climbed up into a bunch of olive trees. The driver played his horn round each bend. Then, on a perilous slope, the car stopped. The driver turned in his seat, searching back over his great soaked shoulder as though prepared, even expecting, to find his passengers gone.

'La Caporale,' he said.

The woman bent, peering out of the car windows. She could see nothing but stones and grass. The heat seized the stationary taxi, turning it into a furnace.

'But – where?'

He indicated something which she could not see, then hauled himself out of the driving seat, lumbered round and opened the door.

'*Ici?*' she asked, absolutely disbelieving.

He nodded, spoke, again waved an arm, pointing.

'*Mais . . .*' It was no good. 'He says we're here,' she told the child. 'We'd better get out.'

They stood on the stony ground, looking about them. There was a black barn, its doors closed. There was a wall of loose rocks piled together. The cicadas screeched. There was nothing.

'But where's the house?' she demanded. 'Where is the house? *Où est la maison?*'

The driver picked up their suitcases and walked away. She took the child's hand, pulling him after her. The high heels of her sandals twisted on the hard rubble; she hurried, bent from the waist, as though on bound feet. Then, suddenly remembering, she stopped and pulled out of her large new handbag a linen hat. She fitted this, hardly glancing at him, on the child's head. 'Come on,' she said. 'I can't think where he's taking us.'

Round the end of the wall, over dead grass; and above them, standing on a terrace, was the square grey house, its shuttered windows set anyhow into its walls like holes in a warren. A small skylight, catching the sun, flashed from the mean slate roof.

They followed the driver up the steps on to the terrace. A few pots and urns stood about, suggesting that somebody had once tried to make a garden. A withered hosepipe lay on the ground as though it had died trying to reach the sparse geraniums. A chipped, white-painted table and a couple of wrought-iron chairs were stacked under a palm tree. A lizard skittered down the front of the house. The shutters and the doors were of heavy black timber with iron bars and hinges. They were all closed. The heat sang with the resonant hum of failing consciousness. The driver

6

put the suitcases down outside the closed door and wiped his face and the back of his neck with a handkerchief.

'*Vous avez la clef, madame?*'

'*La clay? La clay?*'

He pursed and twisted his hand over the lock.

'Oh, the key. No. *Non*. Monsieur and Madame Gachet . . . the people who live in the house . . . *Ce n'est pas,*' she tried desperately, '*ferme.*'

The driver tried the door. It was firm. She knocked. There was no answer.

'*Vous n'avez la clef?*' He was beginning to sound petulant.

'*Non. Non. Parce que* . . . Oh *dear.*' She looked up at the blind face of the house. 'They must be out. Perhaps they didn't get my wire. Perhaps . . .' She looked at the man, who did not understand what she was saying; at the child, who was simply waiting for her to do something. 'I don't know *what* to do. Monsieur and Madame Gachet . . .' She pushed back her damp hair. 'But I wrote to them weeks ago. My husband wrote to them. They *can't* be out.'

She lifted the heavy knocker and again hammered it against the door. They waited, at first alertly, then slackening, the woman losing hope, the driver and the child losing interest. The driver spoke. She understood that he was going, and wished to be paid.

'But you can't leave us like this. Supposing they don't come back for hours? Can't you help us to get in?'

He looked at her stolidly. Furious with him, humiliated by his lack of chivalry, she ran to one of the windows and started trying to prise the shutters open. As she struggled, breaking a fingernail, looking about for some object she could use, running to her handbag and spilling it out for a nail file, a pair of scissors, finding nothing, trying again with her useless fingers, she spoke incessantly, her words coming in little gasps of anger and anxiety.

'Really, one would think that a great man like you could *do* something instead of just standing there, what do you think we shall *do*, just left here in the middle of nowhere after we've come all this way. I can tell you people don't behave like this in England, haven't you got a knife or something? *Un couteau? Un* couteau, for heaven's sake?'

She was almost hysterical. The driver became angry. He picked up her wallet, thrown out of the handbag, and shook it at her. He spoke very quickly. Frightened, she controlled herself. She snatched the wallet from him. She was trembling.

'Very well. Take your money and go.' She had not got the exact amount. She gave him ten thousand francs. He nodded, looked over the house once more, shrugged his shoulders and moved away.

'The change!' she called. 'Change . . .' pronouncing the word, with little hope, in French. '*L'argent* . . .'

'*Merci, madame,*' he said, raising his hand. '*Bon chance.*'

He disappeared down the steps. In a moment she saw him walking heavily, not hurrying, across the grass.

'Well,' she said, turning to the child. 'Well . . .' She paused, listening to the taxi starting up, the sound of its engine revving as it turned in the stony space, departing, diminishing – gone. The child looked at her. Suspicion, for the first time in his life, darkened and swelled his face. It became tumescent, the mouth trembling, the eyes dilated before the moment of tears.

'Let's have some chocolate,' she said. The half bar fallen from her handbag, had melted completely. 'We can't,' she said, with a little, brisk laugh. 'It's melted.'

'Want a drink.'

'A drink.' As though in a strange room, she looked round searching for the place where, quite certainly, there must be drink. 'Well, I don't know . . .' There was a rusty tap in the wall, presumably used for the hose. She pretended not to have seen it. Typhus or worse. She remembered the grapes – they looked far from ripe – that had hung on sagging wires over the steps. 'We'll get into the house,' she said, and added firmly, as though there were no question about it, 'We must get in.'

'Why can't we go into the house?'

'Because it's locked.'

'Where did the people put the key?'

She ran to the door and started searching in the creeper, along the ledge, her fingers recoiling from fear of snakes or lizards. She ran round to the side of the house, the child trotting after her. A makeshift straw roof had been propped up over an old kitchen table. A rusty oil stove stood against the wall of the house. She searched in its greasy oven. She tried the holes in the wall, the dangerous crevices of a giant cactus. The child leant against the table. He seemed now to be apathetic.

'We'll go round to the back,' she said. But at the back of the house there were no windows at all. A narrow gully ran between the house and a steep hill of brown grass. The hill, rising to dense woods, was higher than the roof of the house. She began to climb the hill.

'Don't come,' she called. 'Stay in the shade.'

She climbed backwards, shading her eyes against the unbearable sun. The child sat himself on the wall of the gully, swinging his legs and waiting for her. She looked down on the glistening roof and saw the small mouth of the skylight, open. She knew, even while she measured it with her eyes, imagined herself climbing through it, that it was inaccessible. Her mind gabbled unanswerable questions: how far is the nearest house? Telephone? How can we get back to Nice? Where does the road lead to? As she looked down at the house, something swift and black, large as a cat, streaked along the gutter, down the drainpipe and into the gully.

'Johnny!' she called. 'Johnny!' She began to run back down the hill. Her ankle twisted, she fell on the hard grass.

She pulled off her sandals and ran barefoot. 'Get up from there! Don't sit there!'

'Why?'

'I saw . . .'

'What? What did you see?'

'Oh, nothing. I think we'll have to go back to that house we passed. Perhaps they know . . .'

'What did you see, though?'

'Nothing, nothing. The skylight's open.'

'What's a skylight?'

'A sort of window in the roof.'

'But what did you *see*?'

'If there was a ladder, perhaps we could . . .' She looked round in a worried way, but without conviction. It was to distract the child from the rat.

'There's a ladder.'

It was lying in the gully – a long, strong, new ladder. She looked at it hopelessly, disciplining herself to a blow from fate. 'No,' she said. 'I could never lift it.'

The child did not deny this. He asked. 'When are the people coming back?'

'I don't know.'

'I want some chocolate.'

'Oh, Johnny!'

'I want a drink.'

'Johnny – *please*!'

'I don't want to be at France. I want to go home now.'

'Please, Johnny, you're a big man, you've got to look after Mummy—'

'I don't *want* to—'

'Let's see if we can lift the ladder.'

She jumped down into the gully. The ladder was surprisingly light. As she lifted one end, propping the other against the gully wall, juggled it, hand over hand on the rungs, into position, she talked to the child as though he were helping her.

'That's right, it's not a bit heavy after all, is it, now let's just get it quite straight, that's the way . . .'

Supposing, she thought, the Gachets come back and find me breaking into the house like this? You've paid the rent, she told herself. It's your house. It's scandalous, it's outrageous. One must do *something*.

'Are you going to climb up there?' the child asked, with interest.

She hesitated. 'Yes,' she said. 'Yes, I suppose so.'

'Can I go up the ladder too?'

'No, of course not.' She grasped the side of the ladder firmly, testing the bottom rung.

'But I *want* to . . .'

'Oh, *Jonathan*! Of course you can't!' she snapped, exasperated. 'What d'you think this is – a game? Please, Johnny, *please* don't start. Oh, my God . . .' I *can't* face it, she thought, as she stepped off the ladder, pulled herself up on to the grass, held his loud little body against her sweat-soaked blouse,

12

took off his hat for him and stroked his stubbly hair, rocked him and comforted him, desperately wondered what bribe or reward she might have in her luggage, what prize she could offer . . . She spoke to him quietly, telling him that if he would let her go up the ladder and get into the house she might find something, she would almost certainly find something, a surprise, a wonderful surprise . . .

'A toy.'

'Well, you never know.' She was shameless. 'Something really *lovely*.'

'A big toy,' he stated, knowing his strength.

'A big toy, and a lovely bath and a lovely boiled egg—'

'And a biscuit.'

'Of course. A chocolate biscuit. And a big glass of milk.'

'And two toys. One big and one little.'

'Yes, and then we'll go to sleep, and not tomorrow but the next day Daddy will come . . .' She felt by the weight against her breast, that she was sending him to sleep. She put him away from her carefully. He lay down, without moving the curled position of his body, on the grass. He sucked his thumb, looking at her out of the corners of his bright eyes. 'So I'll climb the ladder. You watch. All right?'

He nodded. She jumped down into the gully again, pulled her tight skirt high above her knees, and started to climb. She kept her eyes away from the gutter. The fear of a rat running close to her made her sick, almost demented with fear. If I see a rat, she thought, I shall jump, I know

I shall jump, I can't face it. She saw herself lying dead or unconscious in the gully, the child left completely alone. As she came level with the roof she heard a sound, a quick scuttering; her feet seemed steeped in hot glycerine, her hands weakened. She lay for a moment face downwards on the ladder, certain that when she opened her eyes she would be falling.

When she dared to look again, she was amazed to see how near she was to the skylight – little more than a yard. This distance, certainly, was over burning slate, much of it jagged and broken. But the gutter was firm, and the gradient of the roof very slight. In her relief, now edged with excitement, she did not assess the size of the skylight. The ladder, propped against the gully wall, was steady as a staircase. She mounted two more rungs and cautiously, with one foot, tested the gutter. Now all she had to do was to edge, then fling herself, forward; grasp the sill of the skylight and pull herself up. She did this with a new assurance, almost bravado. She was already thinking what a story it would be to tell her husband; that her daughters – strong, agile girls – would certainly admire her.

She lay on the roof and looked down through the skylight. It was barely eighteen inches wide – perhaps two feet long. She could no more get through it than a camel through a needle's eye. A child, a thin child, could have managed it. Her younger daughter could have wormed through somehow. But for her it was impossible.

She looked down at the dusty surface of a chest of drawers. She could almost touch it. Pulling herself forward a little more she could see two doors – attics, no doubt – and a flight of narrow stairs descending into semi-darkness. In her frustration she tried to shake the solid sill of the skylight, as though it might give way. It's not fair, she cried out to herself; it's not fair. For a moment she felt like bursting into tears, like sobbing her heart out on the high, hard shoulder of the house. Then, with a kind of delight, she thought – Johnny.

She could lower him through. He would only have to run down the stairs and unbolt one of the downstairs windows. A few weeks ago he had locked himself in the lavatory at home and seemed, for a time, inaccessible. But she had told him what to do, and he had eventually freed himself. Even so, I don't believe you can do this, she told herself. I don't believe you can risk it. At the same time, she knew that she had thought of the obvious – it seemed to her now the only – solution. Her confidence was overwhelming. She was dealing with the situation in a practical, courageous way. She was discovering initiative in herself, and ingenuity.

She came quickly, easily down the ladder. The boy was still curled as she had left him. As she approached, smacking the dust and grime from her skirt, he rolled on to his back, but did not question her. She realised with alarm that he was nearly asleep. A few minutes more and nothing would rouse him. She imagined herself carrying him for miles along the road. Already the heat was thinning. The cicadas, she noticed, were silent.

'Johnny,' she said. 'Would you like to climb the ladder?'

His eyes focused, but he continued to suck his thumb.

'You can climb the ladder, if you like,' she said carelessly.

'Now? Can I climb it now?'

'Yes, if you want to.'

'Can I get through the little window?'

She was delighted with him. 'Yes. Yes, you can. And, Johnny . . .'

'What?'

'When you've got through the little window, I want you to do something for me. Something very clever. Can you do something clever?'

He nodded, but looked doubtful.

She explained, very carefully, slowly. Then, taking his hand, she led him round to the front of the house. She chose a window so near the ground that he could have climbed through it without effort from the outside. She investigated the shutters, and made certain that they were only held by a hook and eyelet screw on the inside. She told him that he would have to go down two flights of stairs and then turn to the right, and he would find the room with the window in it. She tied her handkerchief round his right wrist, so that he would know which way to turn when he got to the bottom of the stairs.

'And if you can't open the window,' she said, 'you're to come straight back up the stairs. Straight back. And I'll help you through the skylight again. You understand? If you can't open the window, you're to go *straight back* up the stairs. All right?'

'Yes,' he said. 'Can I climb the ladder now?'

'I'm coming with you. You must go slowly.'

But he scaled it like a monkey. She cautioned him, implored him, as she climbed carefully. 'Wait, Johnny. Johnny, don't go so fast. Hold on tightly. Johnny, be *careful* . . .' At the top, she realised that she should have gone first. She had to get round him in order to reach the skylight and pull him after her. She was now terribly frightened, and frightened that she would transmit her fear to him. 'Isn't it exciting?' she said, her teeth chattering. 'Aren't we high up? Now hold on very tightly, because I'm just going to . . .'

She stepped round him. It was necessary this time to put her full weight on the gutter. If I fall, she thought clearly, I must remember to let go of the ladder. The gutter held, and she pulled herself up, sitting quite comfortably on the edge of the skylight. In a moment she had pulled him to her. It was absurdly easy. She put her hands under his arms, feeling the small, separate ribs. He was light and pliable as a terrier.

'Remember what I told you.'

'Yes.' He was wriggling, anxious to go.

'What did I tell you?'

'Go downstairs and go that way and open the window.'

'And supposing you can't open the window?'

'Come back again.'

'And hurry. I'll count. I'll count a hundred. I'll go down and stand by the window. You be there when I've counted a hundred.'

'All right,' he said.

Holding him tightly in her hands, his legs dangling, his shoulders hunched, she lowered him until he stood safely on the chest of drawers. When she let go he shook himself, and looked up at her.

'Can you get down?' she asked anxiously. 'Are you all right?'

He squatted, let his legs down, slid backwards on his stomach and landed with a little thud on the floor.

'It's dirty down here,' he said cheerfully.

'Is it all right, though?' She had a new idea, double security. 'Run down those stairs and come back, tell me what you see.'

Obediently, he turned and ran down the stairs. The moment he had gone, she was panic-stricken. She called, 'Johnny! Johnny!' her head through the skylight, her body helpless and unable to follow. 'Come back, Johnny! Are you all right?'

He came back almost immediately.

'There's stairs,' he said, 'going down. Shall I go and open the window now?'

'Yes,' she said. 'And hurry.'

'All right.'

'I'm beginning to count now!' And loudly, as she slid back to the ladder, she called, 'One ... two ... three ... four ...' Almost at the bottom, her foot slipped, she tore her skirt. She ran round to the front of the house, and as she came up to the window she began calling again in a bold voice, rough with anxiety, 'Forty-nine ... fifty ... fifty-one ...' She hammered with her knuckles on the shutter, shouting, 'It's this window, Johnny! Here, Johnny! This one!'

Waiting, she could not keep still. She looked at the split in her skirt, pushed at her straggled hair; she banged again on the shutters; she glanced at her watch; she looked up again and again at the blank face of the house.

'Sixty-eight ... sixty-nine ... seventy ...!'

She sucked the back of her hand, where there was a deep scratch; she folded her impatient arms and unfolded them; she knocked again, calling, 'Johnny! Johnny! It's this one!' and then, in a moment, 'I've nearly counted a hundred! Are you there, Johnny?'

It's funny, she thought, that the crickets should have stopped. The terrace was now almost entirely in shadow. It gets dark quickly, she remembered. It's not slow. The sun goes, and that's it: it's night-time.

'Ninety ... ninety-one ... ninety-two ... Johnny? Come on. Hurry up!'

Give him time, she told herself. He's only five. He never can hurry. She went and sat on the low wall at the edge of the terrace. She watched the minute hand of her watch creeping across the seconds. Five minutes. It must be five minutes. She stood up, cupping her hands round her mouth.

'A hundred!' she shouted. 'I've counted a hundred!'

An aeroplane flew high, high overhead, where the sky was the most delicate blue. It made no sound. There was no sound. As though she were suddenly deaf she reached, stretched her body, made herself entirely a receptacle for sound – a snapping twig, a bird hopping; even a fall of dust. The house stood in front of her like a locked box. The sunlight at the end of the terrace went out.

'Joh-oh-oh-nny! I'm here! I'm down here!'

She managed to get two fingers in the chink between the shutters. She could see the rusty arm of the hook. But she could not reach it. The shutters had warped, and the aperture at the top was too small for anything but a knife, a nail file, a piece of tin.

'I'm going back up the ladder!' she shouted. 'Come back to the skylight! Do you hear me?'

One cicada began its noise again; only one. She ran round to the back of the house and for the third time climbed the ladder, throwing herself without caution on to the roof, dragging herself to the open skylight. There was a wide track in the dust, where he had slid off the chest of drawers.

'Johnny! Johnny! Where are you?'

Her voice was deadened by the small, enclosed landing. It was like shouting into the earth. There was no volume to it, and no echo. Without realising it, she had begun to cry. Her head lowered into the almost total darkness, she sobbed, 'Johnny! Come up here! I'm here, by the skylight, by the little window!'

In the silence she heard, quite distinctly, a tap dripping. A regular, metallic drip, like torture. She shouted directions to him, waiting between each one, straining to hear the slightest sound, the faintest answer. The tap dripped. The house seemed to be holding its breath.

'I'm going down again! I'm going back to the window!'

She wrestled once more with the shutters. She found a small stick, which broke. She poked with her latchkey, with a comb. She dragged the table across the terrace and tried, standing on it, to reach the first floor windows. She climbed the ladder twice more, each time expecting to find him under the skylight, waiting for her.

It was now dark. Her strength had gone and her calls became feeble, delivered brokenly, like prayers. She ran round the house, uselessly searching and shouting his name. She threw a few stones at the upper windows. She fell on the front door, kicking it with her bare feet. She climbed the ladder again and this time lost her grip on the gutter and only just saved herself from falling. As she lay on the roof she, became dizzy and frightened, in some part of her, that she was going to faint. The other part of her didn't care. She lay for a long time with her head through the skylight, weeping and calling, sometimes weakly, sometimes with an attempt at command; sometimes, with a desperate return of will, trying to force herself through the impossible opening.

For the last time, she beat on the shutters, her blows as puny as his would have been. It was three hours since she had lowered him through the skylight. What more could she do? There was nothing more she could do. At last she said to herself, something has happened to him, I must go for help.

It was terrible to leave the house. As she stumbled down the steps and across the grass, which cut into her feet like stubble, she kept looking back, listening. Once she imagined she heard a cry, and ran back a few yards. But it was only the cicada.

It took her a long time to reach the road. The moon had risen. She walked in little spurts, running a few steps, then faltering, almost loitering until she began to run again. She remembered the pink house in the vineyard. She did not know how far it was; only that it was before the woods. She was crying all the time now, but did not notice it, any more than she was aware of her curious, in fact alarming, appearance. 'Johnny!' she kept sobbing. 'Oh, Johnny.' She began to trot, keeping up an even pace. The road rose and fell; over each slope she expected to see the lights of the pink house. When she saw the headlamps of a car bearing down on her she stepped into the middle of the road and beat her arms up and down, calling, 'Stop! Stop!'

The car swerved to avoid her, skidded, drew up with a scream across the road. She ran towards it.

'Please! . . . Please! . . .'

The faces of the three men were shocked and hostile. They began to shout at her in French. Their arms whirled like propellers. One shook his fist.

'Please . . .' she gasped, clinging to the window. 'Do you speak English? Please do you speak English?'

One of the men said, 'A little.' The other two turned on him. There was uproar.

'Please. I beg of you. It's my little boy.' Saying the words, she began to weep uncontrollably.

'An accident?'

'Yes, yes. In the house, up there. I can't get into the house—'

It was a long, difficult time before they understood; each amazing fact had to be interpreted. If it had been their home, they might have asked her in; at least opened the door. She had to implore and harangue them through a half-open window. At last the men consulted together.

'My friends say we cannot . . . enter this house. They do not wish to go to prison.'

'But it's *my* house – I've paid for it!'

'That may be. We do not know.'

'Then take me to the police – take me to the British Consul—'

The discussion became more deliberate. It seemed that they were going to believe her.

'But how can we get in? You say the house is locked up. We have no tools. We are not—'

'A hammer would do – if you had a hammer and chisel—'

They shook their heads. One of them even laughed. They were now perfectly relaxed, sitting comfortably in their seats. The interpreter lit a cigarette.

'There's a farm back there,' she entreated. 'It's only a little way. Will you take me? Please, please, will you take me?'

The interpreter considered this, slowly breathing smoke, before even putting it to his friends. He looked at his flat, black-faced, illuminated watch. Then he threw the question to them out of the corner of his mouth. They made sounds of doubt, weighing the possibility, the inconvenience.

'Johnny may be dying,' she said. 'He must have fallen. He must be hurt badly. He may' – her voice rose, she shook the window – 'he may be dead . . .'

They opened the back door and let her into the car.

'Turn round,' she said. 'It's back there on the left. But it's away from the road, so you must look out.'

In the car, since there was nothing she could do, she began to shiver. She realised for the first time her responsibility. I may have murdered him. The feeling of the child as she lifted him through the skylight came back to her hands: his warmth. The men, embarrassed, did not speak.

'There it is! There!'

They turned off the road. She struggled from the car before it had stopped, and ran to the front door. The men in the car waited, not wishing to compromise themselves, but curious to see what was going to happen.

The door was opened by a small woman in trousers. She was struck by the barrage of words, stepped back from it. Then, with her myopic eyes, she saw the whole shape of distress – a person in pieces. 'My dear,' she said. 'My dear . . . what's happened? What's the matter?'

'You're English? Oh – you're English?'

'My name's Pat Jardine. Please come in, please let me do something for you—' Miss Jardine's handsome little face was overcast with pain. She could not bear suffering. Her house was full of cats; she made splints for sparrows out of matchsticks. If her friend Yvonne killed a wasp, Miss Jardine turned away, shutting her eyes tight and whispering, 'Oh, the poor darling.' As she listened to the story her eyes filled with tears, but her mind with purpose.

'We have a hammer, chisel, even a crowbar,' she said. 'But the awful thing is, we haven't a man. I mean, of course we can try – we *must* try – but it would be useful to have a man. Now who can I—?'

'There are three men in the car, but they don't speak English and they don't—'

Miss Jardine hurried to the car. She spoke quietly but passionately, allowing no interruption. Another woman appeared, older, at first suspicious.

'Yvonne,' Miss Jardine said, breathlessly introducing her. 'Get the crowbar, dear, and the hammer – and perhaps the axe, yes, get the axe—' At the same time she poured and offered a glass of brandy. 'Drink this. What else do we need? Blankets. First-aid box. You never know.'

'Thank you. Thank you.'

'Nonsense, I'm only glad you came to us. Now we must go. Yvonne? Have you got the axe, dear?'

The three men had got out of the car and were standing about. They looked, in their brilliant shirts and pointed shoes, their slight glints of gold and chromium, like women on a battlefield – at loss. Yvonne and Miss Jardine clattered the great tools into the boot. Miss Jardine hurried away for a rope. The men murmured together, and laughed quietly and self-consciously. When everything was ready they got into the car. The three women squeezed into the back.

On the way, driving fast, eating up the darkness, Miss Jardine said, 'But I simply don't understand the Gachets. If they knew you were coming today. I mean, it's simply scandalous.'

'They are decadent people,' Yvonne said slowly. 'They have been spoiled, pigging it in that house all winter. The

26

owners take no interest, now their children are grown up. The Gachets did not wish to work for you, obviously.'

'But at least they could have *said*—'

'They are decadent people,' Yvonne repeated. After half a mile, she added, 'Gachet drinks two litres of wine a day. His wife is Italian.'

Now there were so many people. The hours of being alone were over. But she could not speak. She sat forward on the seat, her hands tightly clasped, her face shrivelled. When they came to the turning she opened her lips and took a breath, but Miss Jardine had already directed them. They lurched and bumped up the lane, screamed to a stop in front of the black barn doors.

'Is that locked too?' Yvonne asked.

There was no answer. They clambered out. Yvonne gave the tools and the rope to the men. Yvonne and Miss Jardine carried the blankets and the first-aid box. The moonlight turned the grass into lava.

'A torch,' Miss Jardine said. 'Blast!'

'We have a light,' the interpreter said. 'Although it does not seem necessary.'

'Good. Then let's go.'

She ran in front of them, although there was no purpose in reaching the house first. It was so clear in the moonlight that she could see the things spilled out of her handbag, the mirror of her powder compact, the brass catch of her purse. Before she was up the steps she began to call again, 'Johnny? Johnny?' The others, coming more slowly behind her with their burdens, felt pity, reluctance and dread.

'What shall we try first? The door?'

'No, we'll have to break a window. The door's too solid.'

'Which of you can use an axe?'

The men glanced at each other. Finally the interpreter shrugged his shoulders and took the axe, weighing it. Yvonne spoke contemptuously to him, making as though to take the axe herself. He went up to the window, raised the axe and smashed it into the shutters. Glass and wood splintered. It had only needed one blow.

She was at the window, tugging at the jagged edges of the glass. The interpreter pushed her out of the way. He undid the catch of the window and stood back, examining a small scratch on his wrist and shaking his hand in the air as though to relieve some intolerable hurt. She was through the window, blundering across a room, while she heard Miss Jardine calling, 'Open the front door if you can! Hold on! We're coming!'

They did not exist for her any longer. She did not look for light switches. The stairs were brilliant.

'Johnny?' she called. 'Johnny? Where are you?'

A door on the first-floor landing was wide open. She ran to the doorway and her hands, without any thought from herself, flew out and caught the lintel on either side, preventing her entrance.

He was lying on the floor. He was lying in exactly the same position in which he had curled on the grass outside, except that his thumb had fallen from his mouth; but it was still upright, still wet. His small snores came rhythmically, with a slight click at the end of each snore. Surrounding him was a confusion, a Christmas of toys. In his free hand he had been holding a wooden soldier; it was still propped inside the lax, curling fingers. She was aware, in a moment of absolute detachment, that the toys were very old; older, possibly than herself. Then she stopped thinking. She walked forward.

Kneeling, she touched him. He mumbled, but did not wake up. She shook him, quite gently. He opened his eyes directly on to her awful, hardly recognisable face.

'I like the toys,' he said. His thumb went back into his mouth. His eyelids sank. His free hand gripped the soldier, then loosened.

'*Jonathan!*'

With one hand she pushed him upright. With the other, she hit him. She struck him so hard that her palm stung.

One of the women started screaming, 'Oh, no! . . . No!'

She struggled to her feet and pushed past the blurred obstructing figures in the doorway. She stumbled down the stairs. The child was crying. The dead house was full of sound. She flung herself into a room. 'Oh, thank God,' she whispered. 'Oh, thank God . . .' She crouched with her head on her knees, her arms wrapped round her own body, her body rocking with the pain of gratitude.

SATURDAY LUNCH WITH THE BROWNINGS

Madge Browning lay, stiffly curled, in bed. Her back was turned to her husband, but she knew he was awake. The sun poured already through the thin curtains and down in the garden the children were shouting. She could distinctly hear the grating of the iron swing, the thud of a rubber ball on the stone paving. If only once, she thought, we needn't be woken up at seven. The thought lay, tranquil, in her mind and drifted down, slowly left her, to join the rest of her extraordinary waking thoughts, the forgotten sediment of every day.

'Are you going to get up?' she asked, not turning.

'Hell, it's Saturday.' He flung his arm across her, pinning her down.

'I don't see what difference it makes.' Because he stayed at home all the time, a writer, a man lacking the mystery of someone who comes and goes, she could never see why he cared so much about Saturday. Her previous husband had left the house five mornings a week at eight and come home five evenings a week at seven. On Saturdays he had worn different clothes. William wore the same sort of clothes all the time. His life was without punctuation, a steady repetition of the same thing.

'What's so special,' she asked, tugging the bedclothes away from him, 'about Saturday?'

'You know I can't work with the children about the place.'

'I don't see why you have to work on Saturday. Other men don't.'

'You spend money,' he said, 'whatever day of the week it is.'

'All right. I'm sorry. Perhaps you'd like me to take them out for the day. We could sit in the park, I suppose.'

'Don't be silly.' His hand moved heavily to her thigh. They lay in silence, both listening to the children, the distant clatter of breakfast being prepared in the kitchen.

'What's the plan?' he asked at last.

'What plan?' She was being deliberately stupid. He meant, she knew, what had she arranged for them today, this compulsory holiday; what had she provided for their entertainment, what meals, expeditions, security from disturbance.

'Well, what's happening?'

At last she turned, looked at him. He was thirty-seven, but in bed he looked older, the thin hair straggled over his forehead, the face heavy and loose like an old man. In the eight years of their marriage, forced to support two step-children and one of his own, he had become successful and careless. His fingernails were dirty and he hadn't shaved for two days.

'Bessie's going to a party this afternoon.'

'That's good.' Bessie was his own child, his darling. He had a great affection for good-humoured, untidy, sexy women with undistinguished names. His daughter was everything he loved. The possibility of her being unhappy tormented him. The idea of her being happy, admired, invited out to tea in her pink net and coral necklace, was a personal compliment. He found it hard to realise that Madge played any real part in her life.

'I wish they'd ask Rachel too,' Madge said. 'It's so bad for her to be left out.'

'Why should they ask Rachel?'

'Well, she knows the Bernsteins just as well as Bessie does. Perhaps I'll phone. I'm sure they wouldn't mind.'

'I don't see why Rachel should have to do everything Bessie does. She's got her own friends.' He flung back the bedclothes and was stamping, with long, hairy, bare legs, about the bedroom. 'Rachel's two years older than Bessie. They've got to lead their own lives.'

'Yes,' Madge said. 'All right.' Saturday had begun, the day of the children. She lay uncovered, exposed, her arms limp by her sides, her head turned sideways on the pillow, eyes closed.

'Well,' he asked, 'aren't you going to get up?'

'Yes. In a minute.'

'Rachel can go next door and watch television,' he said, pausing, looking down at her.

'I know.'

'Melissa can take her to the park.'

'Perhaps.'

'Well, then, aren't you going to get up?'

The day had already been picked up, aimed and thrown towards evening; it soared from the firm ground of sleep, a world on its own.

Madge never went down to breakfast. She refused, out of a strong feeling of self-preservation, to acknowledge its existence. William's temper was unreliable in the early morning, and particularly on Saturdays, with Rachel and Bessie lolling about in a holocaust of cornflakes and burnt toast, the German maid reading letters from home while the coffee boiled dry and the neighbouring children, small, ugly and savage, standing in a row outside the french windows watching him eat, a curiosity which they observed once a week, swarming over the low walls dressed for holiday in feathers, jeans and their mothers' broken jewellery.

This morning there were five of them. The day was going to be warm and the windows were open on to the tiny garden which was already littered with tricycles and dolls, an empty bottle and two saucepans. The five neighbours stood motionless listening to William eating his bacon. He had already told them three times to go away.

'Move,' he insisted mildly. 'Go away. Off with you.'

They glanced at each other, then back to him, their eyes steady, impassive.

'Tell them to go away,' he hissed at Rachel. 'They're your friends.'

'They aren't,' she said coldly. 'They're Bessie's.'

'They aren't,' Bessie retorted.

'I don't care whose friends they are. Just tell them to go away.'

'Actually,' Rachel said, 'they aren't anybody's friends.' She bent again over her book of Bible stories, her thin shoulders hunched, absently cramming her mouth with toast.

'You're not supposed to read at meals,' Bessie said. 'Is she?'

'I've told you to tell them to go away,' William snapped. He had known Rachel all her life; as a small baby, she had gone with Madge and himself on their honeymoon. She had cried the whole time. He had never forgiven her. She bit her nails and still, at the age of nine, wet her bed; she was skinny and spiteful and clever, with a great burden of love inside her, a heart too passionate and heavy for her flimsy little body. Her lank, whitish hair was held back by a pink plastic slide and her small, pale eyes moved busily over the story of Abraham. She didn't answer.

William leant over and took hold of the book. Her hands tightened. They both pulled at it vigorously.

'Will you do as you're told?'

'Stop it! Stop it!'

'Give me that book.'

The five neighbours watched, impartial. Bessie slowly spread another piece of toast. The book ripped in half and Rachel, in an agony of grief, was pounding the floor.

'It was a library book,' she howled. 'You beast, you beast, you beast.'

'Perhaps it will teach you to do as you're told!' In his dressing gown and bare feet, brandishing a crumpled picture of Moses in the bullrushes, he felt foolish and unhappy. Why did his days have to begin like this? What had he done to deserve it? What the hell was it all for? He looked down at the hysterical child, rocking her half of the book as though it were dead, performing, in miniature, all the extravagant gestures of tragedy.

'Oh, shut up,' he said wearily. 'I'll buy you another book.'

He left her howling in the wreckage, watched dispassionately by Bessie and the neighbours, and climbed slowly upstairs.

• • •

His wife was getting dressed. On Saturdays, like the children, she wore different clothes. Today, for some reason, she was putting on a kind of haymaking costume, jeans and a checked shirt, and her hair tied back with a bow.

'Well,' she asked, 'what was all the noise?'

'What noise?' In need of comfort, he came behind her and clamped his hands over her breasts, leaning heavily against her.

'Rachel was screaming.'

'Rachel's always screaming.'

She hardened, moving away from him. He lumbered after her, persistent.

'Kiss?'

'Oh, William, for heaven's sake.'

'All right. I'm sorry.'

She began stripping the bed. She always turned the mattress on Saturdays.

'Why don't you go and work up in Melissa's room?' she asked, heaving at blankets. 'You wouldn't hear them there.'

'I don't want to work in Melissa's room.'

'All right, then, don't.'

'I ought to have an office.'

'You say that every Saturday. Every single Saturday. Why don't you get one?'

He took the other side of the mattress and helped her to turn it. She began making the bed again, patting and smoothing and tucking like a hospital nurse.

'Buzz, buzz,' he said. 'Busy little bee. I think I'll go back to bed.'

'Now,' she said. 'Don't start.'

'I'm not starting.' He searched round for something to attack her with. 'I suppose Melissa's not up yet?'

'I don't expect so.'

'Why don't you make her get up?'

'Yes, darling.'

'Why should she stay in bed, just because it's Saturday? Why doesn't she get up and help a bit?'

'As it happens,' Melissa said from the doorway, 'I'm up.' She stepped over the pile of blankets and walked, with a perfected swivelling motion, to the long mirror at the other side of the room. There, faced with her own remarkable image, she turned and twisted, picking off a few pieces of fluff, patting the shining pony tail of hair, baring her teeth, pulling her belt one hole tighter. Then, apparently satisfied, she rotated back across the room, stepped over the blankets and went away.

William looked sharply at his wife. She was smiling towards the empty doorway; the smile turned towards him, including him in love. He tried to find some response in himself, but it wouldn't come. He left her and went to his study and sat down at his desk and looked straight in front of him, at nothing. In the garden immediately below his window Rachel and Bessie and the five neighbours were squirting each other with the garden hose. Each time they screamed, he flinched.

By lunch time, after buying Rachel a new book and having a couple of stiff whiskies in the pub, he felt better. If we can get through lunch, Madge thought, we shall be all right. She beamed at him encouragingly as he picked up the carving knife and fork. It was at times like this, when they were all together and relatively peaceful, that she almost felt they might make a success of it. She had given William roots, set him at the head of a family table, given him something to work for; she had given her own children a home and a father. The picture was as clear, as static and lifeless as a Victorian print of domestic bliss. It was her ideal, doggedly worked for. That, she had told herself, the strong, wise, loving father, is William; those devoted, secure, happy children are ours; that beautiful, gentle, capable mother might, with a stretch of the imagination, be me. This is Saturday Lunch with the Brownings.

'Bessie,' she said softly, 'sit straight. And do stop sucking your knife.'

'Well,' William said, beaming round over the hot mutton, 'this is all very pleasant.'

'You say that every Saturday,' Melissa sighed. 'And I'm not, actually, slimming.' She leant over and helped herself to another potato.

'I don't want any cauliflower,' Rachel whined.

'You must have some.' William slapped a large spoonful on her plate. 'Makes your hair curl.'

'It doesn't and I hate it.'

'Eat it up,' he snapped.

'The Phillips's rang,' Madge said desperately, 'and asked us for a drink on Thursday. Melissa, pass Daddy the salt.'

'Good.' He settled in his chair. 'What time has Bessie to be at the Bernsteins'?'

'About three.'

'Why can't I go?' Rachel demanded, hitting her cauliflower with her fork. 'It's not fair.'

'Because you haven't been asked,' William said. 'And for heaven's sake stop messing about with that cauliflower.'

'Well, really!' Melissa muttered.

'What did you say?'

'Nothing.'

'Why doesn't Melissa take her to the park?' William suggested blandly.

'Because I've got to do my homework.'

'You can do your homework tomorrow.'

'I can't.'

'Why not?'

'Because I'm going out tomorrow, if you must know.'

William looked across the table at his wife. 'Why,' he asked, 'is Melissa in such a bad temper?'

She tried to send him an urgent, soundless message across the table. Please, she implored him, please stop it. He looked at her blankly, awaiting an answer to his question.

'You could go next door and watch television,' she pleaded. 'Couldn't you, Rachel?'

'You're always telling me it's bad to watch television. You just want to get rid of me, that's all.' Overwhelmed by this thought, at last put into words, the child's face darkened, her mouth sagged, she began, loudly, to cry.

'Oh, God,' William said, 'the child's impossible.'

'She's not!' Melissa flared. 'She's perfectly reasonable! Just because you pick on her all the time.'

'Be quiet!' Madge didn't realise she had shouted until the sound, harsh and violent, slapped across the room. The children stared at her. After a moment's silence they began eating again, warily.

'Well,' William said, when it had sunk in, 'there's no need to shout.'

'I'm not,' she said quietly, trembling, 'shouting. Melissa, will you clear away the plates?'

The danger seemed to be past. It had been, at least, no worse than most Saturday lunches. They all relaxed. Bessie knelt on her stool and put her elbows on the table. Melissa turned sideways in her chair, her back to William, crossing her elegant legs. William lit a cigarette. Madge

41

divided a bowl of cherries with scrupulous fairness among the three children.

'I love cherries,' Rachel said gratefully.

'Well,' William said, 'don't spit the stones out on to your plate.'

'Where shall I spit them, then?'

'Into your hand.'

'Bessie's spitting hers out on to her plate,' Melissa said distantly.

'Then she mustn't.' Tenderly, he leant over and hung four branched cherries over Bessie's ears. She smiled, blushing with pleasure.

'Look, Rachel. Do they look pretty?'

Rachel nodded and eagerly hung cherries over her own ears. The two children shook their heads and bobbed about, stretching their faces and rolling their eyes.

'Haw, haw, haw,' said Rachel, in a plummy Lady Bountiful voice. 'And how are you this morning, Miss Browning?'

'Oh, I'm very well, thank you,' Bessie said, pushing out her stomach and jerking from side to side on her stool. 'See you later, Alligator.'

'See you in a little while, Crocodile.'

'Oh, eat them up,' William said wearily, 'for heaven's sake.'

Rachel, beside herself, screwed up her face and stuck a branch of cherries between her nose and upper lip, 'See you later, Alligator,' she mumbled. Bessie doubled up with laughter. Melissa and her mother sat with patient, distant looks waiting for the exhibition to be over; weakly, they even smiled. William turned his back on Rachel, grinding his cigarette into the empty cherry bowl. A man who can't even hang cherries on his own daughter's ears without hell being let loose, he thought. Never able to do anything simple, eat a straightforward meal, play with my own child, without that skinny little bitch ruining it all.

'My God,' he shouted, 'eat up those bloody cherries and behave yourself. Melissa, why the hell don't you start washing up?'

Melissa got up and very quickly, very quietly, began clearing the table. Bessie climbed on William's knee, locked her arms round his neck. Reluctantly, like a girl giving back borrowed jewels, Rachel took the cherries off her ears and laid them reverently in her plate.

'Can I finish them in the garden?' she asked.

'No,' William said, 'you can't.' He pulled Bessie closer to him, burrowing his face into her hot, haystack hair.

Madge, as was her habit after Saturday lunch, went upstairs alone to the sitting room. She never argued with William in front of the children. It was part of the picture. She raged inside herself, and trembled, and often wept. But she had created him as Melissa's and Rachel's father and he must, therefore, be beyond reproach. There must be no disloyalty. She sat on the low windowsill and looked down at the garden. Melissa came out and shook the table-cloth in the sun. She could not even tell Melissa about her anxieties because Melissa, though nearly sixteen, must be secure, must feel her parents united, must be happy. Her love for Melissa, older and stronger than any other love, was not part of the picture; it could suffer change and movement and was the only thing, perhaps, in her life which would remain with her till her death. Nevertheless, she kept distant from her, afraid of factions, unfairness, any kind of turbulence.

William is a good writer, she thought. It's funny he doesn't understand things. She leant against the low balus-trade outside the window, listening to the subdued clatter of washing up. Sunlight glinted on the tin and chromium of abandoned toys on the lawn and three sparrows were pecking among the crumbs shaken off the tablecloth. The neighbours seemed to be already asleep, their gardens deserted.

Rachel ran outside, holding her hands together. Quick, neat as a little rat, she folded herself up in the corner of the wall, in the shadow. She opened her hands and a bunch of cherries fell into her lap. She began to eat them, quickly, tearing off the stalks with her teeth and spitting out the stones, her eyes on the dining-room window.

After a few minutes Bessie came out and sat on the swing.

'Daddy said you weren't to eat your cherries in the garden,' she called in a friendly way. 'Rachel's eating her cherries in the garden.'

William came out of the house and walked across the lawn. He walked slowly, unaware that he was being watched by his wife. Rachel did not move, pressed back against the wall. He took hold of her wrist and pulled her to her feet. Automatically, she began to cry, loud, ugly wails. It's right, Madge thought remotely, he did tell her not to eat cherries in the garden. They walked back across the lawn and into the dining room, the man dragging the little girl by the wrist. Bessie began to swing higher, the iron frame shaking.

For another moment, there was silence. Perhaps, Madge told herself weakly, it will be all right. A cat prowled along the wall and someone far along the street turned their radio on, a thin whine of music. Then there was a crash, a splintering of china.

'Stop it!' Melissa was screaming. 'Stop it! Stop it!'

He's hurting Melissa, Madge thought. At one moment she thought this, standing in the sun with the cat just turning the corner by the laburnum tree. At the next she was already downstairs, fighting with teeth, nails, kicking, shaking the unresisting, heavy body, hammering his head against the table, sobbing, shouting. 'You hit my children, you hit my children,' and all the time, remote and cool in the back of her mind, the certainty that this was the end, death, that after this there could be nothing.

Bessie watched from the window. She did not understand until it was over. Then, without moving, she began to cry. Rachel had been crying all the time. Now she stopped, edging back towards Melissa. The two adults stood in the centre of the room, dishevelled, breathing quickly and loudly, their eyes riveted to each other. The small sound of Bessie's crying meant nothing to them. They were, for the first time in their life together, alone.

'You hit my children.' She repeated the statement again and again. 'You hit Melissa. Get out.'

'You think I won't get out?' His face was grey, bloated with anger. 'You think I'd stay with you and these delinquent little bitches of yours? Get their father to keep them. Go on, go and find him. Tell him to keep the lot of you on his five pounds a week. I'm taking Bessie and I'm getting out. I'm taking Bessie.'

He grabbed the child's hand and pulled her out of the room. The sound of her crying increased, became desperate, as he dragged her up the stairs. Melissa had disappeared. Rachel and her mother looked at each other over the wrecked dining room, the overturned table, the spilled and dying flowers.

'Can I go to the party?' Rachel asked. 'Instead of her?'

Upstairs, in the high, hot bedrooms, William was packing. He did not for a moment let go of Bessie's hand, but pulled her rapidly from place to place, in and out of the bathroom, her bedroom, his own room. She ran and stumbled behind him, blind with crying.

'Which is your favourite dress? You can take it. Which is it?'

'I don't know!'

One-handed, he pulled a couple of dresses off their hangers, hurried her back to the bedroom, bundled them into the suitcase.

'Not another minute,' he said. 'You don't stay one minute with them. You'll live with me. I'll look after you. Stop crying. Which is your toothbrush?'

'I don't know!'

'Stop crying. What are you crying for?'

'I want to go to the party!' She was shaking convulsively, her few teeth chattering. 'I want to—'

'There'll be plenty of parties. Blow your nose.'

'But I want—'

She saw her mother come into the room. Her mother looked tall and cold, like a ghost. She wrenched away from her father and flung herself at her mother.

'Go and wash your face,' Madge said. 'Then you can put on your party frock. It's almost time.'

'She isn't going to the party,' William said.

'She is my child,' Madge said, her voice flat and tired.

47

'She is going to wash her face and brush her hair and put on her dress and go to the party.'

He stared hopelessly at Bessie. 'Don't you want to come with me?' he asked. 'Just you and me? No Melissa and Rachel. Just us?'

'I want to go to the party.'

He sat down heavily on the bed, covering his face with his hands. He heard his wife and daughter go away, closing the door quietly behind them. After a little while he lay back on the bed curled up next to the gaping suitcase, sighed deeply and fell asleep.

He slept for four hours. When he woke up the house was silent. He heaved himself up, washed his face in cold water, brushed his hair. Then, still yawning a little, he unpacked the suitcase and pushed it under the wardrobe.

In the next room Rachel and Bessie, bathed and in their pyjamas, were both sitting in Rachel's bed cutting out paper dolls. They looked up calmly as he came in.

'Hallo,' he said.

'Hallo. Look what we got at the party.'

'Very nice. Was it a good party?'

'Quite. Rachel came too.'

'Jolly good.' He yawned, feeling his skin creep. 'Where's Mummy?'

'Downstairs.'

'Well, good night, then. Sleep well.'

Melissa's door, on the next landing, was open. She was hunched over her desk, surrounded by textbooks. The wireless was on and the room was tidy, smelling strongly of furniture polish.

'Hallo,' he said. 'How's it all going?'

She looked up, biting the end of her pen. 'Oh, it's you.'

He picked up a film magazine from the bed and flipped through the pages. 'I'm sorry,' he said, 'about all that business this afternoon. Forget it.'

'Oh, that's all right.' She dipped her pen and opened a book, busy, efficient. 'I suppose you don't know anything about the Gulf Stream?'

'Nothing at all.'

He wandered out of the room and down the stairs. The sitting room door was shut. He opened it cautiously. Madge was sitting on the window sill. She was sewing. She had changed her clothes.

'Hallo,' he said.

She didn't answer.

'I've been asleep,' he said.

She bit off the cotton, put the needle in the pincushion, folded the skirt she had been mending and put it on one side.

'Funny thing,' he said. 'I went out like a light. How do you feel?'

She had clasped her hands and he saw the nails whiten as she pressed her fingers together.

'What's happening?' he asked. 'What's the plan?'

She turned her head away sharply. He sat down on the other end of the window seat.

'I've made it up with Rachel and Melissa,' he said. 'I suppose it's going to take a good deal longer with you.' A huge boredom at the prospect filled him, weighed him down. He could hardly move his lips to speak. 'Well,' he said, 'I suppose we can just sit here.'

With a great effort, he lifted his hand and let it fall on her knee. She sat rigid, as though movement might break her to pieces, staring out over the darkening gardens.

SUCH A SUPER EVENING

The important thing about this story, really, is not the Mathiesons, but us. Most people know about the Mathiesons. Nobody knows about us, although I think there are a lot of women who might easily be mistaken for me, and, quite honestly, it often takes me a moment or two to recognise Roger in a crowded room. This, of course, could never happen to the Mathiesons, who are recognised by everybody as being themselves. I get in an awful muddle when I try to explain things like this, so perhaps I'd better just get on with it.

Roger was called to the Bar in 1947, just a year after he came out of the Army. Of course, I didn't actually know him then; in fact, I was still at school – Cheltenham, actually – and we didn't meet until Daddy and Mummy brought me up to London for my coming-out. They were frightfully impressed by Roger, who really did seem to have awfully good prospects, and, to cut a long story short, we had a sweet wedding and a small marquee for the reception, and after a while, when we knew we weren't going to have any children, Roger managed to get this rather quaint flat in the Temple. Of course, Daddy and Mummy were frightfully impressed by that, too – our names painted on the door, and such delightfully high ceilings. They are too old to come from Gloucestershire now, and anyway, they're as poor as church mice, poor darlings, taxed out of existence. Perhaps this is just as well, since Roger shows no sign whatever of becoming Lord Chancellor, and Mummy has given up all hope and sent my doll's house to a jumble sale.

Well, this story really begins last spring, just after our tenth wedding anniversary. Of course, when you have been married to anyone for ten years you're bound to feel just the slightest bit restless. There must have been an urge somewhere deep down in Roger to change our lives, although goodness knows I never dreamt he had urges at all, of any sort. I knew I had, because I often found I was feeling sorry for myself, and although I kept telling myself I was a silly muggins, it just didn't work. Then I would snap at Roger and . . . well, then I would be sorry for Roger, too. Although not, perhaps, in the way he wanted me to be.

• • •

Nothing ever quite came off, that was our trouble. Roger had a nice, steady practice, but we all knew he was no Marshall Hall. We were quite well off, I suppose, but nothing ever seemed to wear out – I suppose because Mummy had told me so often that a piece of good tweed is worth its weight in gold, and of course a little Chippendale chair or a mahogany sideboard simply goes on forever. I had a kind of awful suspicion that we could be more friendly with our friends than we actually were, and certainly that Roger and I could be *more* married, although I couldn't imagine how. We had quite a full social life, of course. We went out at least once a fortnight – sherry or bridge or the occasional *fondue* party. People liked us. I wouldn't say they were wildly enthusiastic, but they did like us. There was never quite enough of anything, that's what it was. You always felt as though you could manage a penny bun, as nanny used to say.

I don't know if I was feeling this more than usual that afternoon. I think I must have been, otherwise I wouldn't remember it so clearly. Roger had just gone back to Chambers after lunch. He only has to walk about two hundred yards – not counting the stairs, because we live on the fourth floor – to his chambers, but he always wears his bowler hat and carries his umbrella. It was a beautiful spring day, and I stood by the window and watched him hurrying off, so anxious not to be late. A few barristers were creeping round the garden, taking the sun, and Harrods had just delivered my library books. Roger always turned the wireless on for the one o'clock news, but when he left I switched it over to *Woman's Hour*. What with *Woman's Hour* and a few library books and a little knitting, it's quite possible to pass an afternoon, even in the Temple. I was just looking forward to this, in a hopeless sort of way, when Mrs George Bulmer telephoned and asked us to a party to meet the Mathiesons.

I'm taking it for granted, of course, that you know about the Mathiesons. But since it's just possible that there are people who don't – lighthouse men, or men who have spent the last five years on some ice floe or something – I had better explain why this was one of the most exciting things that had ever happened to me.

The Mathiesons were – and, I suppose, still are – an institution. They symbolise a whole way of life. First of all, they had these eight children. Their marriage, I suppose, partly because of this, was continually being referred to by bishops and magistrates and even the occasional High Court judge. Why, they kept asking us all, can't you live like the Mathiesons? As though that wasn't enough, they were both fantastically successful writers, and Felicity had just made quite a stir with a small exhibition of action paintings – which I confess we hadn't seen, although we kept meaning to. The energy of those two was absolutely staggering. They wrote novels (Felicity's were slimmer and printed on thicker paper, and I'm sorry to say Roger found them rather hard going) and television plays and radio plays and stage plays – in small theatres with small casts and often accompanied by concrete music – and criticism of practically everything, and short stories and memoirs and children's books, and even, occasionally, poetry. They wrote film scripts and commentaries and librettos of one or two curiously savage operas. They gave long, amusing interviews to the Press, and if ever a newspaper wanted to find out about children watching television, or the teenage problem or how to run a house on thirty shillings a week, they got on to the Mathiesons straight away. And the Mathiesons always managed to say the right thing – intelligent, but human – progressive, but somehow cosy. You loved them all – all ten of them – and the great thing was that it was *right* to love them. You weren't, as Roger might say, letting the side down or being vulgar or anything. Their children – Sophia, Simon, Emma, Henrietta, Sebastian, Philippa, Piers and the baby, Adam – were not at all like other people's children. They had great personality and even, in a way, dignity. Well, of course, this is how their parents wrote about them, and you can't tell much from photographs, particularly in the newspapers. Anyway, they were obviously remarkable children. Being Mathiesons, they could hardly help it.

I don't think there was anybody in the world I wanted to meet more. I'm not a terribly excitable person, but at that moment I felt exactly as though I was Cinderella and

Mrs George Bulmer was my fairy godmother (awfully silly, I know, because actually I didn't like her very much, she is the mother of a barrister called George Bulmer, who is rather an odd young man). So glad you could come at such short notice, she said – don't dress up, dear, simply come in any old thing, about nine. Then she rang off.

Now, I'm not the sort of person who possesses 'any old thing'. I am not at all sure what it means, and the idea of it makes me very nervous. Did she mean the little black with or *without* pearls? I couldn't ring up anyone to ask, in case they hadn't been invited, so in the end I rang up Roger, who was in the middle of a conference and not frightfully helpful. I suppose by the time he came home I was a little nervy, and of course spreading his briefs all over the table didn't help, since we had to dine early, so we were a little sharp with each other. I made an omelette and a green salad – I adore cooking, by the way, it takes up so much time – and Roger rather sweetly opened a bottle of wine, although I seldom drink at home unless we have people to dinner. When I put on my black (with pearls) it suddenly looked dreadfully *triste*, and something frightful had happened to my hair – perhaps it was nerves, or the spring or something. Never mind, I remember thinking, no one will notice me, anyway. I'm often cruel to myself in order to be kind. Sometimes at the Pegasus Ball or something

56

like that I go to the Ladies and make dreadful faces at myself in the mirror so that my ordinary face, the one I go back into the room with, would seem quite glamorous to people, if only they'd seen the other ones.

In the end, of course, we arrived far too early. I always mean to tell Roger that this sort of party starts an hour later than the time we're asked for, but I hate deceiving him. He's dreadfully unhappy if he thinks we aren't punctual, and I do like him to be happy, even if it makes me suffer. I think one of the strongest things I feel for Roger is a kind of anxious sympathy. It's difficult to describe and may be what mothers feel about their children. I don't know. Anyway, the first two hours of Mrs Bulmer's party were so dreadful that even my anxiety for Roger wouldn't have stopped me from going and sitting in the bathroom if the Mathiesons – just at the crucial moment – hadn't arrived.

Now, I had seen them once on television – in Harrods, actually, we didn't have it in the flat then – and of course I had seen their pictures hundreds of times. But I was still quite staggered to see how handsome they were. He was a big, well-built man with the sort of face that used to belong to matinée idols – more intelligent, of course, but still at its best in profile. She was tiny and slim and blonde and had that sort of hair style that looks as though you've just stepped out of a storm and enjoyed it. I remember thinking

57

she was like a little doll and it was absolutely fantastic to think she had those eight children. Although I no longer wanted to hide in the bathroom after they came in, I was terrified at the idea of actually meeting them. Of course, I didn't think for one moment we would meet them. We were supposed to be just part of the scenery.

Roger knew this perfectly well, and what came over him I shall never know. Of course, I said at the beginning that he may have felt an urge to change our lives, but there's a lot of difference between feeling an urge and actually doing something about it. Possibly he had drunk too much – he does, I confess, drink rather enthusiastically at times. Anyway, at one moment we were standing in our corner looking brightly around and trying to think of something to say to each other – and at the next he had left me, simply abandoned me without a word of warning, without a drink or anything to do with my hands (except put on my gloves which looks absurd in the middle of a party), and was making a beeline for the Mathiesons. By the time I had got over the shock and elbowed and apologised after him and got practically submerged, and struggled on, using Philip Mathieson's profile as a beacon, and finally landed up wedged behind Roger and quite unable to make myself felt, let alone heard . . . well, it was all over. They both, Roger and Philip Mathieson, were scribbling in their diaries – Mathieson, I remember, with a gold fountain pen. Roger had asked the Mathiesons to dinner.

That was how it happened, and that was what occupied our lives for the next three weeks. Or rather, my life. Men, of course, are different. It wasn't, it really wasn't, just that I wanted to score over Mrs George Bulmer – who had treated us *very* strangely, as though we had been guilty of frightfully poor taste, like rising from the dead or something – or to impress our friends. Although our friends were, I must admit, impressed. No – it was much more than that. When I thought that *we* were going to be friends of the Mathiesons I felt (I don't know) that all the dreams I had had at Cheltenham might, after all, come true . . . I forgot all about the Pegasus Ball and the Bar Point-to-Point and my grief that Roger always backs the horse that won't start, and that I feel I'm too old to learn the cha-cha, and that when we die there will be nobody to be sorry . . . Perhaps I even thought that by having the Mathiesons to dinner I was going to experience, myself, a small part of their lives. Have just a small part of one child, for instance (I preferred, of all of them, Philippa), or write one line of a book. I don't know. I felt that after they had been to the flat, and we had talked to them, we might be able to live – how can I explain? – altogether more *bravely* . . . In the meanwhile, I confess, I was simply terrified.

Our first problem was – who to invite with them? Roger said we must have someone, but the more I thought of our friends the more I thought it would be better to have the Mathiesons by themselves. Roger, however, asked the Plunkett-Williams without even consulting me, and the first thing I heard of it was a breathless telephone call from Miriam asking what she should wear and could I lend her Felicity's last book because there was a waiting list at the library, and so on. I was simply livid. In fact, I could hardly bear to speak to Roger the whole evening. Edgar Plunkett-Williams is a barrister in Roger's Chambers, and he and Miriam have two children and live in a very cold little house in W8. I simply couldn't see what they would have in common with the Mathiesons, and I'm afraid, for once, I said so.

It was very odd, the change in us over those three weeks. Every evening Roger seemed to have grown a little balder, and I noticed that the pullover I had knitted for him for Christmas had shrunk, so that when he was sitting down, it crept up over his stomach like a baby's vest. I don't know why this suddenly irritated me. He began to look at me in a strange way, too. For the first time I felt he was watching me eat. Knowing someone is watching the way you eat, makes you feel like something in the zoo. It seems to take hours to finish a mouthful, and when you swallow, it's like gravel. I noticed what a lot of time he spent doing nothing – literally just sitting in the armchair after dinner doing nothing. When we first married he used to be drafting petitions and affidavits and advices on evidence and heaven knows what half the night, and now I wondered how he expected to get anywhere when he just did nothing all the time. Then it occurred to me that he didn't expect to get anywhere, that he was perfectly happy to stay where he was, and this was even worse. I wanted to shake him, and yet I told myself he hadn't changed, he had been like this for years. I was wrong. He was changing even faster than I was, but in secret, deceitfully. He just went on sitting there doing nothing, and all the time he was changing like some dreadful caterpillar pretending to be a twig.

The night before the dinner party, I was tired. We had cold meat for dinner because I was tired. After he had watched me gulping it down for a few minutes, he asked me what the matter was. I said I was tired. He said, in a curiously stiff voice: 'What on earth have you got to be tired about?' I pointed out rather sharply that although he might not have noticed it, the entire flat had been spring-cleaned.

'And supposing,' he sneered, 'you had eight children to look after and a novel to write and were to appear on television tonight *and* had to do the spring-cleaning? I suppose that would be a little too much for you? I suppose that would be entirely beyond your powers?'

It was really so perfectly beastly – and so terribly unexpected – that I just stared at him and burst into tears. He was breathing heavily through his nose, which he always does when he feels anything strongly. He simply got up from the table and settled himself in the armchair and started reading the *Spectator*, and didn't speak another word to me. It was our first real quarrel and I hope we never have an evening like that again. Quarrels are horrible to people like us; it's only very unusual people who manage to turn them into sort of ornaments which they feel undressed without.

Of course if this story weren't true – if it were written by one of the Mathiesons, for instance – they would have forgotten to come, or put it off at the last moment, and there we should have been the next evening with the dinner all ready and the ice in the Martini jug, left high and dry in our own little world, staring into a vaguely disagreeable future. I admit I had moments during the day when I thought it wasn't true – or even, in spite of everything, wished it wasn't. They arrived, in fact, just as the clock struck eight – before the Plunkett-Williams and before Roger had got the ice out of the refrigerator.

'Are we too early?' Felicity asked, and stepped inside, glowing.

'We thought it would be hard to find,' Philip said. 'But it was surprisingly easy.'

And I said to myself well, it's begun. And I said to Roger – we hadn't spoken since the outburst the night before – 'Would you get the ice, darling?' My voice sounded as though it had been recorded under rather bad conditions – muzzy and distant and over-refined. Felicity curled up in Roger's armchair and said, 'What a perfectly wonderful room,' and Philip, standing in front of the fireplace and patting the backs of his trouser legs said, 'I say what a super flat this is.'

I thought the word 'super' was only used by children in books, so I laughed rather heartily without quite knowing why. Felicity took a packet of cigarettes out of her handbag and I offered her one of ours and she said oh well, they were all the same, she'd have one of ours later. I was so concentrated on this sort of thing, and the thought of the dinner, that I didn't really notice anything else.

At last – I suppose they were really only ten minutes late – the Plunkett-Williams arrived. Miriam was wearing chandelier earrings, a mistake really. Roger mixed more drinks and I had one eye on the dinner and the other roaming about for ashtrays and so on. All I realised was that Philip Mathieson was doing most of the talking – thank goodness – and that from the roars of laughter everything was going beautifully.

'. . . A ghastly sore throat,' I gathered, 'and quite unable to move my arm – but not an inch!'

'Which arm?' Miriam inquired, dangling sympathetically.

'His right arm,' Felicity said. 'He should have it insured.'

'Well, as I was going into Television House yesterday, I met this man . . .'

When I came back from the kitchen (I did try to be as unobtrusive as possible about this, but it's not easy), Philip was talking about Income Tax and Roger and Edgar had the expression of men who, after the comic, have been asked to join in a short prayer.

'We've solved it all by having half a dozen companies, the kids are all shareholders and about four of them as secretaries. Last year we whittled our taxable income down to £5,000. Not bad, really. You should try it, Walker.'

'How much,' Roger asked with awe, 'was your gross income?'

'Haven't the faintest idea. What would you say, sweetie? £15,000, £20,000. Something like that. This accountant of mine is about two feet high and wears pince-nez ...' He crouched down, circling his eyes with his fingers and making a small, prissy face. He was really very funny. I thought Felicity was rather quiet, but then, artistic, sensitive women often are. She asked me where the bathroom was, and when she got up, fell over the pouf. It was silly of me to leave the pouf sitting right in the middle of the floor, but I did think it was big enough for anyone to see and not walk straight into, as she did. She said it was quite all right and limped off to the bathroom. Roger watched her until she was out of the room. He looked owlish. I finished his drink, although normally I never drink spirits, they make me silly.

I think I said that I adore cooking, but not that I really specialise in Spanish dishes. This is because for the last seven years we have spent our summer holiday on the Costa Brava. For the first three years of our marriage we went to Lyme Regis, which has no cuisine to speak of – but that's by the way. For this dinner, which I had planned terribly carefully, we started with Huevos Escalfados Madrid-Nieves, which is about as complicated as its name, and not, as Roger says, just a few old poached eggs thrown together. I must say he had taken great pains over the wine – I mean there seemed to be a lot of different shaped bottles – and there were green and white candles on the table. The room had great dignity, in a draughty sort of way.

'You *must* all come down to Gumble,' Philip Mathieson said impulsively. 'We've bought this vast mansion, you know, just ten miles north of Scarborough.'

'An architectural nightmare,' Felicity cut in suddenly. 'It was built in 1802 and—'

'There's this super great banqueting hall—'

'With a minstrel's gallery. And you have no idea – the *statues*!'

'Surrounded by twenty acres of parkland—'

'No, darling. Only ten.'

'Twenty. It stretches right over to Little Gumble.'

'Little Gumble is only a mile and a half away, and the boundary on the other side—'

'My dear girl, Little Gumble is at least three miles away. Has anyone got an Ordnance Map of Yorkshire?'

Nobody had.

'Anyway,' Philip said, 'you start off on the ground floor with this huge banqueting hall . . .'

I took the plates away and Roger filled their glasses. When I brought in the Riñones de Carnero a la Señorita and the Escalibada, they were just finishing a tour of the kitchens and going up the main staircase.

'It must be wonderful,' Miriam said, rather bravely I thought, 'for the children.'

'Oh, they just sit glued to television wherever they are. It doesn't make the slightest difference.'

'Mine,' Miriam confided, 'are *much* better than they were. John, he's six, told me the other day, "You know, Mummy, I've got the 'clusion that Pop-Eye is *boring*!" That's rather a step forward, I think, don't you?'

There was a ghastly silence. I have never seen so many stony faces in my life.

'Indeed it is,' I said. The Rinones lacked something, and I thought perhaps it was using frozen and not fresh peas. Felicity left half hers and lit a cigarette from one of the candles. They didn't lack as much as that.

'What I can't understand,' Roger said with dreadful gallantry, filling her glass again, 'is how on earth you manage, I mean, with eight children and everything else.'

'The meals alone,' Miriam sighed. 'Like an army.'

'And to look,' I said, and I didn't really stress the word much, 'so young with it.'

She tapped her ash over her uneaten food and sighed.

'She does it on delicious American pills, specially imported,' Philip said. 'Don't you, darling?'

'One's got to do something,' she moaned softly. 'Otherwise – you know – one would simply wring their necks.'

'And of course she doesn't really see them all that often.'

'I see them a good deal more than you do!'

'I suppose you have help?' Miriam asked, quick as a flash. I really began to feel I had underestimated her.

'Well, we have a nanny and two ghastly Swedes and a cook, if you can call that help.'

'And are any of the children away at school?'

'No. We did try it, but we keep wanting them for one thing or another, and it's such a bore to send reporters and photographers dashing off to Sussex or somewhere. The schools were stupid about it, too. Also they can make the odd ten gins from modelling if they're at home. It all helps.'

Miriam's earrings were quite still, petrified with shock. I cleared away and brought in the Tocinos del Cielo. I'm very proud of these, and perfectly happy to explain how I make them. However, no one seemed to want to know. They were all beginning to look as though they were at a funeral, except for Philip. He was talking about getting away from it all.

'Why not?' he was asking Edgar, who had a dogged expression. 'Throw it all up and go. What keeps us in this bloody country, anyway? I'm seriously considering getting domiciled in the South of France. Now why don't you do that, Walker?'

'I doubt,' Roger said feebly, 'whether there's a Probate, Divorce and Admiralty Division in the South of France.'

'Oh, of course, it's all very well for you boys – half the year off and great fat fees for divorcing your best friends. Take silk, lay down the port, make a good rousing speech now and then. It's the work that's killing me. The rat race.'

Miriam came to life again. 'I read somewhere that you get up at six every morning. That really is . . .'

There was a short, horrifying noise from Felicity. We all stared at her. She hadn't touched her Tocinos.

'You know what time he gets up?' she said pleasantly. 'Midday. Just in time for lunch at the Caprice. Although, of course, there are occasions when he gets up at ten. Then he has to have a snooze in the afternoon.'

'A siesta,' I said stupidly.

'Meanwhile, all those poor little men in Harrow and Welwyn Garden City are working away like beavers, ghosting for Philip Mathieson Productions Limited. Which one of them wrote that bit about you getting up at six? Which one did the piece about how you adore playing with electric trains? He hasn't the faintest idea.'

Well, you can see what it was like. It was like riding a runaway horse, and nothing short of disaster could stop it.

We were hurtling to destruction – or that was how I felt while I fetched the coffee. Roger was pouring out brandy like water, which showed how he was feeling. We all sat down and waited very nervously.

'A perfectly ridiculous thing happened to me yesterday,' Philip said. He was stretched full length on the sofa by now. Roger had to sit on the *pouf* and I was on the floor, which I found a little embarrassing.

'Oh yes?' Edgar asked, yawning politely with his mouth shut. 'And what was that?'

'Some fellow rang me up about this new play of mine – *Death and the Earwig*, it opens next Tuesday, I hope you'll be there. Anyway, he was pretty dim for a reporter, he didn't even know how old the children were. My secretary was out, so I had to waste a valuable five minutes looking it up.'

We hung on his words while he laughed at the absurdity of this.

'Well, finally I traced the information he wanted, and started off the usual thing ... Sophia 20, Simon 18, Henrietta 17 ... And then do you know what he said?' He laughed for at least half a minute, kicking up his heels in a boyish way. We smiled hopefully. 'He said, "Really, Mr Mathieson, you must have developed very *early*!"'

The joke was so rich that for a minute or two he didn't notice how puzzled we were.

'He thought,' he explained patiently, 'that they were all mine. Now I ask you – do I honestly look as old as that?'

We didn't look at each other. We certainly didn't look at the Mathiesons. We must have examined the carpet more minutely during those few seconds than four moth detectors. Then suddenly there was the most frightful scream, and Felicity's coffee cup and brandy glass went flying and there she was having what I supposed was hysterics, crying and beating the chair with her fists and howling and twisting as though someone was trying to hold her down. Which nobody was, because we were all too alarmed, except for her husband, who had covered his face with a cushion and seemed to be feigning dead.

There is nothing much you can do with a woman you don't know very well who is having hysterics. I kept patting the air round her and saying, 'Do something, *do* something,' to Roger, who did nothing. The Plunkett-Williams melted away. I didn't even notice they had gone until ten minutes later. I remember thinking well, if Lord Justice Bridlington could see this. It wasn't kind of me, I know, but it made me feel somehow calm and powerful, as though I was part of the great backbone of sanity which keeps life together – and which Felicity Mathieson had obviously parted with long ago, poor thing. By the time she was quiet enough to be taken to the bedroom, she certainly looked her age, which I suppose wasn't much more than forty, anyway. I felt much older, too, and as for Roger, sitting on the edge of his armchair gloomily waiting for Philip to uncover, he looked a really shattered man, like someone sitting on the side of the road staring at a nasty accident.

They didn't, however, go. Not a bit of it. Felicity came back from the bedroom right as rain – I suppose she had taken some of her imported pills – and Philip sat up and looked about him with a dreadful glint in his eyes. I made some tea, feeling there was some connection between tea and emotional strain, and Philip clapped his hands together with a sort of brisk, bedside manner and said: 'Well, as I was saying, you *must* all come down to Gumble ...' And they were off again on the conducted tour – no explanations, no apologies, nothing, simply two clever robots packed with enough talk for a week, with pauses for clapping or laughter or gasps of horror, whichever it might be.

By half past twelve we had given up asking questions – we were bound to hear all the answers, anyway, like those monkeys who type all the sonnets of Shakespeare, given plenty of time. They were talking even faster and their faces seemed to move less. Roger had quietly read a couple of briefs and I had washed up all the dinner things, although usually I leave them for Mrs MacBride, our darling daily.

'In my opinion,' Philip was saying at half past one, 'the modern teenager is absolutely splendid.'

'I think all girls should be told about sex at a very early age,' Felicity said. 'My own daughters, Sophia, Henrietta, Emma and Philippa, have always been fully aware—'

'Boarding school for boys, perhaps,' Philip said. 'Although I doubt whether my own sons, Simon, Sebastian, Piers and Adam, would agree with me . . .'

At two o'clock Roger suddenly said: 'Do you mind if I go to bed? I have to be in Court at ten, rather a difficult—'

'I've evolved a rather cock-eyed way of sleeping myself,' Philip said, looking keenly at the now empty chair. 'I go to bed at nine, and sleep till midnight, then I get up and work till five, and sleep again till nine.'

'I always tell my daughters,' Felicity said, 'beauty sleep is what counts. That's my only recipe for keeping young. I'm in bed by ten, always in bed by ten. Was it Flaubert or de Quincey who said . . .?'

I was left alone with them. If you think I was just tired, or upset, I haven't succeeded in describing the Mathiesons at all. I was terrified. I hadn't the faintest idea what to do. I thought of slipping out and ringing up to say their children were all dying. But I knew it would be in all the newspapers if I did, and it seemed rather hard on the children, although heaven knows I didn't feel tenderly towards them. The same thing applied to the police, and in any case Roger naturally dislikes being involved in any sort of scandal. The only thing that really would have been any good would have been a couple of strait jackets. They were on to writing now.

'When a tap is turned on,' Felicity said, frowning a little, 'water should come out of it. A tap without water is

72

a lie. Look at *Peter Pan*, perhaps one of the most psychologically exciting works of drama ever to come from an English pen. My husband does use a pen, in fact, but I find a typewriter more sympathetic.'

'And always, of course, use Peterson's Ink. I find it smooth, clear, and – a great consideration with eight children in the house – washable.'

They couldn't stop. Nothing could stop them. I stood up and said very loudly, 'I am going to bed.'

'You were saying just now,' Philip said, 'that Little Gumble is only a mile and a half from Gumble Hall. Honestly, you know, you're wrong.'

'I *promise* you,' Felicity said desperately, with a nasty shake in her voice, 'it's only a mile and a half. That copse on the other side of the river—'

I went to bed. I don't know what else I could have done. Our bedroom is a large, rather gaunt room next to the sitting-room. Roger was lying on his back, staring up at the ceiling.

'They're still here,' he said, as though I didn't know.

'What can I do?' I asked humbly.

He thought for a long time. 'Nothing you can do,' he said, 'I suppose they'll go some time.'

I got into bed, and we lay side by side, listening. The sound of their voices went on, rising and falling without a break. Roger was as tense as I was. Suddenly a terrible thought struck me.

'I don't think,' I whispered, 'that they've even noticed we're not there.'

Roger was silent for a long time. I thought he might have gone to sleep, and turned over to look at him. I couldn't bear him to go to sleep. I was really frightened.

He took my hand and squeezed it hard. 'I don't think,' he said, 'they ever noticed we were there.'

So we lay holding hands. That was comforting. We didn't say anything else. At last we went to sleep and when I woke up, the first thing I noticed was the silence.

They had gone. Whether they had just run down of their own accord, or whether they had a sort of alarm clock to tell them when to stop, I shall never know. But there was a note left on the mantelpiece. It said: *Such a super evening. Do come down to Gumble Hall some time. We'll ring you. Philip and Felicity M.*

They never did ring us. That's all, really. I read somewhere that Felicity is expecting another baby, which seems rather hard at her age. Roger and I have decided that since there's only the two of us we might try Yugoslavia in the summer, for a change. It might even come off – you never know. But I'm a great deal more tolerant than I used to be, and even if it does turn out to be the Costa Brava again – well, we shall be together; and very contented, very grateful for each other, in our quiet way.

THE KING OF KISSINGDOM

I was a late child, born when my parents were both in their mid-forties. In the month of my birth my elder brother, then five, was sent to boarding school; the eldest had already been away for some years and was to me no more than an impression of grey-flannel violence, a pair of stocky knees, a whiplash decapitating nettles and the – to me – inaccessible, blowing bells of hollyhocks. The brother who was sent away because of my arrival, obliterated himself. A small, pale, trembling child, I first remember him with a red tape tied round his arm, being sick behind the summer-house. This must have been a day or so before the beginning of a school term, for he hated school with all the passion in his unhappy nature, and never forgave me for it.

In the holidays these brothers, when not Boy Scouting in shaky huts built of evergreen, or marching with heavy rifles on some manikin military manoeuvre, stayed with one or other of our grandmothers. They returned home, always, for the last dreadful days, during which I would become ill, or run away or drop my spectacles down the well – anything to distract the household from its morbid concentration on these two ill-fitting, ill-fitted strangers. The eldest twisted my arm. My other brother seldom spoke to me. When I saw him being sick, in secret, I would never tell anyone: not out of loyalty but because, I suppose, I hoped he might die there behind the summer house or water butt, or hidden in the ferny depths of the herbaceous border – die and never be noticed, crumbling away like the blackbirds and frogs I found and buried. I would, I feel sure, have dug him in beside them with equal ceremony.

I was, then, an only child – an only daughter. The modestly beautiful eighteenth-century house, which my parents had filled with Jacobean furniture, was my home; its garden, my undisputed territory. Alone, I made my country behind the rhododendrons. Here I ate peppery nasturtium leaves and buried my spectacles, for the tenth time, in the loamy earth. I was never unhappy. My parents lived in another world and I do not, for those first seven years, even remember the sound of their voices. The year was always summer, with Christmas suddenly occurring in the middle – and the three uneasy appearances of my brothers, forgotten the moment their trunks and tuck boxes, cricket bats or football boots disappeared from the hall.

This, until the inception of the Little Folks' Nursery, was my land. Beyond the garden gate was a village: but it was almost unknown to me. There was a church, which I visited infrequently, always being hustled out before the sermon. There was 'the big house', owned by the Squire, where once a year, with grizzling reluctance, I went to tea, a clean handkerchief tucked up my knicker leg and always lost. There was the schoolmaster, with his spectacles propped on a rosy, sweating forehead. There was the farmer next door with a beard like Moses and a stomach, I knew, like God. I was frightened of him, but even this was a pleasure. I would crouch on the roof of our tool shed, throwing handfuls of sharp gravel down among his ducks and hens. I was not aware that down in the house, in my father's oak-panelled study, in the great stone-floored kitchen where my mother worked all her life, there was anguish and tragedy – and plans, growing painfully out of these, for my future.

From the tool shed roof, by precariously standing and grabbing, for support, the great branch of a yew tree, I could see the distant orchard. This orchard, which belonged to my father, was on the other side of the road; therefore it was not, in the same way as the garden, my territory. I knew that sometimes, particularly at the end of the holidays when the boys were home, my father would retire there, camping for the day in a disused chicken run. On occasions I would be asked to run over with messages which he received, from his armchair in the chicken hut (he had an oil stove in the winter), or his deck chair among the apple trees, with a vague, bemused smile or a groan of intolerable pain. In either case, I was not tempted to stay. There was nothing, in those days, for me in the orchard. I would avoid, in his affectionate moments, the restraining hand, the encircling arm and skitter back up the orchard, over the gate, scuffing the white dust of the road, back into the garden and home. I never realised that he was lonely.

This was all, until my seventh birthday. I suppose there is some very simple reason why I do not remember the actual process of change, which must indeed have been an upheaval. I do not remember the day the Little Folks arrived, or the building of the Army Hut in the orchard, or the introduction of green baize notice-boards and under-sized desks into my nursery. I do not remember the first time I saw broad beans growing on blotting paper in my own home, or catkins in jam jars or my paintings – of great severity and lack of talent – drawing-pinned to the school-room (no longer nursery) wall. I do not remember the arrival of Miss Briggs. In one dream I was alone on the hot roof, or hidden in the frosty twigs. In the next, without waking, a Little Folk among six other Little Folks, in a house devoted to raw carrot and phonetic spelling; with my father living in the orchard; with Miss Briggs, that timid and beautiful young woman, gently correcting my eating, my speaking, my habits of a lifetime. It happened – and I cannot believe, however hard I try, that I was surprised.

The reasons for the Little Folks' Nursery were practical enough. My father after his retirement had very little money. The house was large and I, they must have thought, was lonely. The Little Folk were children whose parents, for one reason or another, were thankful to be rid of them – Colonial administrators, Empire builders, all sunning themselves in a twilight which they resolutely called high noon. Exotic presents would arrive from India, China, the far flung bazaars of Burma and Malay. The children were yellow and thin, dreadfully overdressed until my mother stripped them of their tweed and flannel and made them deep breathe the English frosts and play naked in the tepid English summers. Their names were Gwen and Brian, Jocelyn and David, Michael and Pamela: mild, English names which suited their delicate natures. I think I felt some pride in their toughening. Affection or resentment did not occur to me.

Was I cruel to them? Do they sicken, even now, in middle age, at the thought of me? I don't know. We slept, the seven of us, in the great bedroom that used to be my father's. All was neat, all was sweetness: we each had our little chair, our little bed, our little tables and our little hymns. My mother, perhaps because of the money, sometimes came out of the kitchen and read to us, in a thrilling, dramatic voice, the Tales of the Norsemen. It was more often winter, with brisk walks in the hard lanes, hips and haws, cold fingers as we drew the holly berry and the redbreast in our Nature books. Miss Briggs changed from cotton to angora, and wore small, childish socks over her stockings. My father lived in the orchard, the Army Hut boiling over like a greenhouse – remote, unknown, left home as far as we knew or cared.

I do not know what went on between my mother, my father and Miss Briggs during the short months of the winter and spring. I can guess, I can imagine: but I do not know, and therefore it is all just as shrouded in mystery to me now as it was that day when we received, for the first time, our invitation to the orchard.

My mother, at this time, must have been in her early fifties – a woman with the fierce, suppressed intensity of a Victorian who had been waylaid, so to speak, by the mild ideals, the sentimental enlightenment of the twenties. She should have attacked, alone with her camel, the Middle East: she should have organised Scutari or poured out, high on some crag or moor, the dark secrets of her strong head and heart: she should at least, at some moment in her life, have chained herself to a railing. Instead of this she had overcome her natural repugnance to ordinary, fallible human nature to the extent of getting married, late in life, and producing three children. This was correct; but it was not, for her, easy. She concentrated her talents on survival;

she fought, every minute of the day, against the slackening
of standards, the easy pull of emotion, the sensuality which
might suddenly arise, an appalling threat, the moment
her back was turned. Hidden somewhere far down in
her complicated personality was a small, rather shocking
talent for laughter, a germ of cruelty, a deep tenderness for
flowers – the only emotion about which she could be artic-
ulate. At the time I sensed some of this, but knew none of it.
To me, not yet grown into the dependence and complicity
of later years, she was my cook and – as far as I possessed
one – my conscience. She was regarded by everyone as a
wonderful woman. I knew this because I was told it, by
the farmer's wife, the schoolmaster's wife, the Squire's
wife, and by the rare, gilded and scented mothers of the
Little Folk, who flashed in and out of our quiet life like
fire-flies. Your mother is a wonderful woman, they said. I
believed them, and still do. But the climate was cold; the
comfort, for a man with so much flesh and blood as my
father, severely disciplined.

Miss Briggs was, I think, nineteen. She seemed to us old
– much the same age, I suppose, as my mother and father.
She was a great deal prettier. She had soft hair, parted in
the middle and coiled in loose, sloppy earphones on either
side of her rather plaintive little face. She had small, thin,
red hands; chapped, no doubt, from her perpetual concern
with botany. I cannot remember that she did any house-
work. Her voice was high and hesitant except when she

sang, when it suddenly increased in volume and became almost robust. 'O Worship the King . . .' she would burst out, energetically conducting with her little red mole's paws, 'All glorious above . . . O gratefully sing, His power and His love . . .' And merrily, heavily, with cheerful rhythm, we would join in, 'Our shield and deFENder, The ancient of DAYS, Pavilioned in SPLENdour and girded with PRAISE . . .' My mother, hurrying past the window with a handful of parsley or mint, some bay leaves tugged from the tough bush, would look at us, it seemed with approval, but without smiling. Was she, perhaps, imprisoned in her kitchen, wistful? At night she came to kiss us good night; but it was Miss Briggs we called back again and again, on various wild pretexts, until she blushed and laughed and patted her sliding earphones and breathed, 'I must go . . . I must go . . .' as though we had captured her.

Once, on an autumn evening – a bonfire was still smouldering – I saw from our dormitory (no longer bedroom) window my father and Miss Briggs walking in the garden. I remember this only because I had not seen my father for some time, and it seemed to me that he had grown smaller than I remembered. They were walking slowly round and round the tennis court with its two blackened posts, its net taken in for the winter, the chalk lines mere smudges on the damp grass.

'Miss Briggs is out in the garden,' I said.

Nobody answered. They were not very receptive children.

'She's all by herself,' I said. 'Walking round the tennis court.'

Nobody proved me wrong. I watched for a little while, more curious to see my father on our land, broken out of his reserve, than I was to find out why they were walking together in the dense October evening. Then I went to bed and forgot it. The next day he was back in the orchard and Miss Briggs taught us a new hymn: Praise my soul the KING of HEAven.

The party, however, came in the summer. The windows were open in the schoolroom and there was pressed groundsel, no doubt, among the blotting paper. We had just had our milk and home-made biscuits and were amusing ourselves, waiting for Miss Briggs to come back and continue our comfortable lessons. Michael was prodding caterpillars – revolting and evil, I thought them – in a jam jar; and Jocelyn, the dainty, was playing with the doll's house my father had made over in his orchard, and had transported by local carrier. We may have been talking, but we seldom said anything of interest or importance. Our conversations were mostly running commentaries on our own activities; the others could listen or not, as they chose.

Suddenly the door opened and Miss Briggs made an entrance. That is, she did not actually come into the room, but stood there, a little breathless, a little pink, clasping a large roll of drawing paper and looking quickly from one to another of her Little Folk. Finally, with a kind of reluctance, she finished up with me: her eyes – large, pale eyes, given to rapid blinking – stayed on my face, and I saw thought moving behind them as one sees weeds, the shadows of weeds, moving in the depths of water.

'Well, children,' she said. It was obviously the beginning of an announcement. We waited. For some reason, I felt uneasy. I wiped my sticky hands on the baggy seats of my shorts; I curled my toes – the first time I remember this secret method of defence, this hanging on – inside my sensible sandals. Miss Briggs was still looking at me. I sniffed, disgustingly, to distract attention. Her eyes whipped away, she was released, she stepped inside the room and closed the door.

'Well, children,' she said, 'I bear an invitation.' She took a deep breath. She was momentarily younger than we were, stammering over her words, overcome with embarrassment. With an awkward movement she held out the roll of paper. 'An invitation,' she said, 'from the King of Kissingdom.'

Our stupidity must have revived her. Since we did not scream, or indeed even move, she briskly unrolled the paper and held it at arm's length. I saw something written in her best noticeboard writing, with Indian ink and a special pen, and a blodge of sealing-wax at the end dropped over a piece of Christmas ribbon. 'Hear ye, hear ye,' she said, and it was her fine hymn-singing voice, 'All faithful subjects of His Affectionate Majesty, the King of

Kissingdom, are bidden to a Royal Banquet at Orchard Palace on this day, the nineteenth day . . .'

The others, I am sure, had no idea what she was shouting about. But I knew, even more certainly than if she had said, 'By the way, your father wants you to go to tea this afternoon.' That might have confused me. This rigmarole, even before it was finished, had pinned me down. Reluctance and dread grew in me, cramped, became a stomach pain. I bolted away, running, my sandals squeaking on the worn, diamond-patterned linoleum. My mother was not in the kitchen. Grated carrot, grated cabbage, nuts and cheese were laid out on a tray; a big earthenware jug of lemonade draped with a muslin cover weighted with small yellow and white beads. I fished a piece of lemon rind out of the jug, sucked it. The sun poured in through the dusty windows, raising the hot smell of coconut matting on damp stone. I threw the lemon rind into the clean sink-basket and, forgetting why I had left, went back to the schoolroom.

The plan, apparently, had been explained. We were to change our clothes, wash our hands and faces, and assemble for a ceremonial march to the Orchard at three o'clock. Until then we were to have a holiday.

We agreed, although I suspect without much enthusiasm. Changes in our routine were not welcome. We seldom had treats, our life being, on the whole, so pleasurable. With the exception of Jocelyn, we hated changing our clothes. I had one dress, made from some sort of folk weave sent from Calcutta. When my mother was cutting it out, she inadvertently pinned the pattern through the material on to a green serge tablecloth. I tried to persuade her to make up the green serge and abandon the folk weave, but without success. The serge was turned into a dozen oven cloths and kettle-holders, brilliantly blanket-stitched by us in Handwork. Nothing was ever wasted.

'But first,' Miss Briggs said – I still detected nervousness in her manner – 'first we must compose our reply, mustn't we? The King has put R.S.V.P. on his invitation. Who knows what that means?'

'It means you've got to answer,' said Jocelyn, the socialite.

'Quite right. So we'll get our paper, our pen, our ink.' Collecting all these things together, Miss Briggs sat down at the table. We gathered round her, with slight curiosity. 'Now what shall we say? To ... His Affectionate Majesty the King of ... Kissingdom ...' The beautiful, flowing script was drawn slowly on to the white paper. Doing this, Miss Briggs bit her lower lip with small, uneven teeth: one earphone tumbled, and she pushed at it impatiently. 'Your faithful subjects accept with pleasure ...'

I was looking out of the window, bracing myself on the window ledge with my hands and letting my legs hang stiffly an inch or two from the floor. I was pretending I had no legs. 'Where's Mummy?' I asked.

'Mummy's out,' said Miss Briggs. 'Now you must all sign.'

'Where's she gone out to?'

'She's gone to London for the day.'

'Why?'

Miss Briggs was seldom irritated. Sometimes, when she had a headache, she sighed. Suddenly, without looking at me, she snapped, 'How should I know why?'

I bumped back on to the floor. The others were silent. 'Now, Jocelyn . . . you sign first. Best writing, mind you.'

One by one, in our spluttering spider handwriting, we signed the acceptance. Miss Briggs was pleased. 'Now we must seal it. Brian, fetch me the sealing-wax. Pamela, bring me the matches off the mantelpiece.' She did not ask me to do anything. I said violently, 'Who's going to get the tea, anyway, if Mummy's not here?'

She turned on me with her pale, sweet eyes and gently took both my hands – her own were not much larger than mine – and clasped me with a cool, damp grip. 'Silly billy,' she said, loving me. 'I'm very good at getting the tea. Aren't you pleased that Mummy's having a holiday?'

I looked at her lap. She was wearing a black and white striped dress, like a camera advertisement. She smelt of Fuller's Earth and a faint tang of sugared violets.

The day continued to be memorable. Miss Briggs was determined on this: nothing was allowed to be ordinary. We had our lunch on the tennis court and were allowed to lie on our stomachs as we ate it. We had chocolate raisins for pudding, washed down with the cold, bitter lemonade. After lunch we were allowed to rest on the bank. Miss Briggs came and read poetry to us. She read 'Up the Airy Mountain' and, as always, I was frightened and moved, burying my head in my arms and blowing gently upwards so that my spectacles became steamed over, and I pretended I was blind. This was more frightening than the poem and I was lost for three or four minutes in terrible self-pity. Miss Briggs looked at me in despair.

'Would you like a ribbon in your hair?' she asked. 'I've got such a pretty ribbon in my room.'

I agreed, although it must have been against my better judgement. I knew she was trying to comfort me. Since I was not, to my knowledge, distressed, the offer of something for nothing was irresistible.

At three o'clock we were all ready. While we were dressing, a high gaiety had come over us; we had strutted about and jumped on the beds and shouted in high, affected voices. But once trussed, buttoned, in white socks and – for those who possessed them – little lockets, we subsided, first into giggles, then into whispers, then into nervous silence. Miss Briggs had changed into a silk print and wore, round her long, pale neck, a string of small pearls. Her earphones were tightened and she wore to our amazement, lipstick. I had never been to the cinema, never seen a magazine; never, I think, ever looked at a newspaper, except the forbidding front page of *The Times* in the days when my father lived at home. The only women I had ever seen to match Miss Briggs that day were the dazzling mothers of the Little Folk; and they, I felt by some curious instinct, were immoral, living behind bead curtains and belonging, no doubt, to the Roman Catholic Church. The effect of Miss Briggs was too successful for open comment. I straightaway refused to look at her. Jocelyn, however, breathed, 'Oh Miss Briggs, you look simply sweet, really you do.' I stumped up to the front of the procession and led the way down the garden path, through the gate, over the sleepy afternoon road. For the first time I remember thinking: I am the daughter of the house.

The orchard was hot and enclosed. I do not remember, as we walked quietly down the path in our white kid sandals and (for the boys) patent leather shoes, whether there was fruit or blossom. I only remember the silence, the rustle of children walking behind me; and over the short, clustered trees a thin spiral of blue smoke, like a camp, that came from my father's chimney-pot. He had made a large clearing round the Army Hut and here I stopped, uncertain, while the children gathered behind me. Apart from the smoke, there was no sign of life. Miss Briggs took charge. She walked – bravely, I thought – to the open door of the hut; we followed, raggedly, a few paces behind.

'O King of Kissingdom,' she called, in her singing voice, 'your faithful subjects have arrived.'

'Enter!' called my father. His voice sounded curiously muffled, as though he were speaking from under the earth.

'Come along, now, children,' she whispered, patting us softly through the door. I was no longer the first. I stumbled over the doormat and pushed clumsily against Michael, who was wearing velvet shorts. At first the comparative gloom of the hut blinded us and we peered, blinking, into a dancing, star-spangled blackness. Then, as the scene began to emerge, we all breathed our 'Ahs' and 'Ooohs' of admiration. I remember, as though this were the first time such a thing had happened to me, smiling.

My father, a large man, was sitting cross-legged on a pile of cushions. He was dressed with a kind of resemblance to Ali Baba and his handsome, heavy face shone with boot polish. He was wearing, on his grey-socked feet, slippers from Madras or Mandalay. The hut was draped with spoils, Indian blankets and cushions from Ceylon; my mother's Spanish shawl served as a tablecloth on the floor, on which was set a glorious tea, spongy and sweet, bright with the frosty green of angelica, the scarlet of pulped tomatoes, the thick brown of relished chocolate, and all on silver dishes, winking and flashing against the scarlet silk. It was a magnificent sight. Unprepared for it, we gaped and gasped. Having smiled, I suddenly felt like crying.

'Welcome, O faithful subjects!' my father boomed. Then, in a slightly different voice, 'Welcome, O Princess Barbara. We trust your journey was without hazard?'

'Quite without hazard, my lord.' This, rather breathlessly, from Miss Briggs. We looked at her with interest.
As Princess Barbara she became even more remote, less of
our world.

'Well, come in, come in,' my father said sharply. 'Don't
all huddle round the door.'

We shuffled forward and, at a nod from Miss Briggs,
squatted on the floor. Of all of them, I was the most shy.
The idea that this radiant sheik, this Emperor of power
and glory, was really my father, was hard to understand. I
had not seen him for some time. Could he, actually, have
changed? Was this how he always lived? Was he really
some Oriental potentate, hidden from me until I was of
an age to understand? Did the village know? A swift
doubt, a chill of apprehension – did my mother know? I
summoned all my courage and said, looking straight at
him, 'We had our rest on the bank.'

He smiled generously. Presumably he recognised me.
'Your rest?'

'And we had our dinner outside, too.'

'Good, good. Now if Princess Barbara will do the
honours ...' He indicated, with a flourish, the silver
teapot, only usually brought out at Christmas. Miss Briggs
knelt next to him on the cushions. As she leant forward
to pour the tea I could see the soft, tender swelling of her
flesh. My father had not boot-polished his hands: square,
stubby and full of strength, they were the only part of him

I recognised. As Miss Briggs passed him his tea, he briefly touched her arm. She got up and came to where I was sitting, kneeling beside me and fussing with the plates. It was very hot in the hut. Her face was pink and her upper lip was pearled with little drops of sweat. I said it was a jolly good tea. She laughed and said magic; it was all, all done by magic.

We demolished the tea leaving only crumbs and sprigs of parsley on the silver dishes. From time to time, momentarily satiated, I risked looking up. My father was in tremendously good humour. He and Miss Briggs kept up the Arabian Nights atmosphere by calling each other, 'O Mighty King' and 'Your Delectable Highness'. As Miss Briggs softly moved about, offering us food, replenishing our cups and glasses, my father followed her with his sharp, bristling blue gaze. Perhaps, like us, he had never seen anything like her before. Once, between the chocolate and orange cakes, I caught his eye, just as it was about to move on. I smiled with all my power, longing, in some way, to congratulate him. His eyes left me, following their trail, up, down, steady, darting, as though Miss Briggs were some rare and restless butterfly. I spilt my tea.

'Oh!' Miss Briggs gasped. 'Your mother's shawl! Quick! Your mother's shawl!' She mopped frantically with a small handkerchief.

'Leave it,' my father said. 'It doesn't matter.'

'Pass the hot water. Pass the hot water.'

There was an anxious scuffle for the hot water jug. Miss Briggs poured a steaming pool over the satin and scrubbed desperately. Her hair was coming loose. I felt sorry for her.

'For heaven's sake,' my father said, 'what does Mabel's shawl matter? Come, come, Princess. A little magic and all will be solved.' He got up and, taking a clean white handkerchief from some hidden pocket, spread it over the stain, intoning, rather wildly, 'Out, out damned spot.' We, who were taught never to say 'dash' or 'crikey', stared at each other.

'But the shawl—!' Miss Briggs wailed, uncomforted.

'Let the dead bury their dead,' my father said. There was an uncomfortable hush. We swung from fantasy to reality as though flying in swing boats. Which was which, we never knew. Let the dead bury their dead. We were abruptly solemn, as though his words had meaning.

'Rise, Princess Barbara, Queen of the apple trees. What do you say, children? Shall we crown her? Shall we say – this is the day of coronation?'

'Yes,' we murmured politely. 'Yes, oh yes, do let's.' But we didn't move. We didn't know how to crown her. Her honours were already too much, beyond our understanding.

'No, Frank, no . . .' she murmured, but he pulled her to her feet among the debris. She whispered: 'Oh, Frank, don't,' but he was too strong for her, dragging her to his throne of cushions. We laughed a little, cruelly eager to see her discomforted. By the time she had plumped on to the floor, one earphone had come down and her dress rode high over her awkward knees. She was pretending, now, to giggle, but I recognised the sound. I said, 'I say, Daddy, but you haven't got a crown.'

'I have everything!' he said, swelling tall and magical. 'I am the King of Kissingdom!' At this, with a splendid gesture, he swept his hand out from the inner folds of his robes; and indeed, he was holding a crown. It was not even cardboard. It was metal, gold, and set with sparkling emerald and ruby. We couldn't believe our eyes. Later, when the crown found its way into our dressing-up box, I realised it was made of a kind of tinfoil. After a number of coronations, less dramatic than Miss Briggs's, it snapped in half and was thrown away. At this moment it was awful, frightening in its splendour. We groaned, hugging our knees, our eyes and mouths wide with a kind of dismay.

'Faithful and loving subjects,' my father said, his voice suddenly quiet, 'do you take Princess Barbara as your Queen, to have and to hold, to love and to cherish, from this day forth and for ever more . . .?'

We were all silent. An imprisoned bee buzzed and banged against a shrouded window. My father's tan was running in great amber drops on to his white robe. He was looking at the top of Miss Briggs's head, holding the crown a few inches above it. I was reminded, terribly, of a picture in my *Child's Guide to History*: the Queen with bowed head, patiently kneeling at the block; the

Executioner waiting, brooding over her braided hair. For many years I thought that Miss Briggs, at this point, had changed into black velvet.

At the moment he touched her with the crown, Miss Briggs burst into tears. The entire spell was broken. We shifted, breathed, recognised each other again. We lost all interest. Michael and Brian even got up and started wandering about, elaborately disassociating themselves from the whole thing. Miss Briggs sobbed, heartbroken, salmon pink, frantically pushing at her nose with the tea-sopped handkerchief. My father stripped off his headdress and threw it into a corner.

'Go on,' he shouted. 'Play! Go outside and play!'

We ambled off, stretching ourselves on the grass outside.

'What shall we play?' Jocelyn asked.

Nobody answered. We were tired out, but curiously contented. I took off my shoes and socks and bound my feet carefully in dock leaves. Brian lay in the fork of an apple tree, stomach down, legs dangling, his cheek pillowed on the rough bark, his eyes shining, staring at nothing. My father's voice came low and steady from inside the hut. Miss Briggs, if she answered, was whispering. Jocelyn plaited grass. The evening shadows grew longer. It did not occur to us to go home. We waited, yawning occasionally, sometimes rolling over or digging absently in the grass with small twigs.

Miss Briggs came out of the hut. She had done her hair, but the impeccable, creamy face had gone. Her face was swollen and shining, like the beginning of measles.

'Come along, children,' she said. 'Best foot forward.'

Silently, we assembled. Brian slipped from his tree; I unwound my bandages; our dresses were stained green, our bows undone. We pulled our clothes away from our sticky skins, rubbed our knees, fell in behind Miss Briggs and left the hut, the orchard, without a backward glance. As we went through the garden gate and were enclosed once more by the high wall, I felt tremendously glad, almost unbearably contented – as though it were I, who had done nothing, who had shepherded them back to safety.

That is all I remember. Miss Briggs left the next day. My mother took us for a picnic and told us not to sit on damp grass. When we returned Miss Briggs had gone. The schoolroom was very tidy, except for one or two hair-pins scattered – probably in her last moments – on the floor. I am sure none of us asked why she had gone. My feeling of responsibility, of grave gratitude, remained for a few days. Shortly afterwards, Miss Field arrived. She was afflicted with a rumbling stomach, had freckles on the backs of her hands, and became a close friend of my mother's. In the evenings, they would walk together in the garden, discussing the roses.

My father came home when the cold set in. He sat in the study again, but slept in an attic, far away from the sound of our morning hymns. I began to know what he looked like, and what to expect from him. We never mentioned the King of Kissingdom. Years later he told me that one night, when I was small, he had been tempted to end his life. But he did not do so. Our lives grew, stretching like shadows thrown by that one long summer.

I TOLD YOU SO

The parents went down the cliff by the path. It was a high cliff, and the path was steep. The concrete slabs that made it were broken and rough. Laura's hands were deep in her coat pockets; her chin was jammed into her collar. She took the great, lolloping strides that were made essential by the steepness of the path and the fact that she was wearing rubber boots. She wheeled the corners on her heel, savagely, with an impression of speed.

Geoffrey followed more cautiously. He was wearing a dark grey suit, because at three o'clock he was catching the train back to London. It was Laura who had insisted that they come to the beach, in order to fill in the hour that remained before it was time to leave for the station. He could have occupied himself perfectly well by reading the Sunday newspapers and checking that he had remembered his razor and toothbrush. As it was, he was certain he had forgotten his razor. Every Monday morning during the past four weeks, he had gone to the office unshaven or unwashed or without a collar stud. He wasn't the type to manage by himself. Laura shouldn't expect it. He worried about this as he picked his way down the path, taking small, sliding steps because of his town shoes. The whole thing made him feel ridiculous.

The three children – Sarah, Catherine, and Angie – had gone off along the cliff edge, looking for some way down more dangerous than the path. They wore red, blue and green jackets. Their heads were swathed in warm angora scarves. They were aimed forward into the wind like figureheads, small and sharp on the horizon on the cliff.

Below, the beach shone enormously with the clear grey light that served on this cold eastern shoulder of England for sunshine. Everything was exactly in focus. The air, without warmth or dust or colour, was strong, but did not taste of the sea. There was a fringe of dry sand just under the cliff, scattered with brittle banana skins and rusty cans, but the rest of the sand, the flat acres of it, was heavy and wet as mud. Castles made of it collapsed like snowmen, and sand puddings, if they turned out at all, were unsatisfactory. The children had long since given up digging.

They came to this part of the beach because it was far enough away from the pier to avoid the deckchairs and bathing huts, the dusty donkeys that ambled with closed eyes backward and forward between the lifeboat and the ice-cream cart. Last weekend, on a freak afternoon without wind, Laura had allowed the children to swim. Geoffrey considered it a miracle they hadn't caught pneumonia. Geoffrey distrusted the North Sea. You could drown in a sea like that, only a few feet from the shore. It had, as he repeatedly told them, treacherous currents. They just stared at him, as though he were teaching them geography instead of trying to protect their lives.

Two or three yards above the beach, the path curved for the last time, taking a gentle gradient behind a few scrubby bushes that grew low on the face of the cliff. Hands still in her pockets, feet together, Laura jumped this small precipice, landing with her boot heels dug into the sand. Without waiting for Geoffrey, she started off towards the sea. He, reaching the beach by the path, plodded after her.

Her jump irritated and saddened him. He knew that it was a gesture – her days were full of them – but what it was meant to represent he had no idea. Why jump, risking a sprained ankle and endless inconvenience, when there was a perfectly good path? Why not hang on his arm, timidly negotiating the bend, the cracks in the concrete slabs, arriving with a little hop, if necessary, on the safer, level ground? They weren't children, to be throwing their bodies carelessly about as though they were of no value. They weren't young, for God's sake.

Laura was diminishing across the huge beach. Her footprints, unnaturally large, disappeared almost immediately in the watery sand.

'Laura!' he shouted. 'Laura!'

She dragged to a standstill, but didn't look round.

'Wait for me!' he yelled plaintively. He did not walk any faster. They were like two reels of cotton; one had unwound to its fullest extent, the other was now wrapping itself, cocoon like, in the taut, extended thread. At last he reached her. 'Don't go rushing off like that. What d'you want to rush off like that for?'

She didn't answer, but moved her shoulders restlessly in the heavy duffel coat. Now he was here, there was no point in walking on. His presence made her realise that there was nowhere to go but the sea. He made her feel that once you had looked at the sea, walked about bravely in its shallows, thrown a pebble or two, there was nothing left to find out about it. She sighed, narrowing her eyes, peering at the distant summit of the cliff. 'Can you see the children?'

His eyes unwillingly scaled the sandy, apparently perpendicular face of the cliff, searching vaguely about on ledges, behind tufts of scrub. 'No. Do you think they're all right?'

'I should think so.'

'I don't think you should let them go off on their own like that.'

'Oh,' she said. 'Don't you?' She began playing noughts and crosses on the sand with the toe of her boot.

She didn't even listen to him anymore. They might not be young, but they were at least married. He had some rights. Did she really think, because she was managing here without him, that he was unnecessary? Unnecessary to her? It was horrible. 'Look,' he said urgently, 'why don't you all come back with me? Now. Today. There's a later train. We could catch it easily.'

She glanced at him before drawing a line through the noughts and crosses. 'Don't be silly.'

'But you've been here a month, for God's sake. You don't know what hell it is in London.'

'Of course it isn't.' She spoke briskly, in the same way she told the children how tremendously they enjoyed school. Then, looking up, she said with pleasure, 'Oh, there they are.'

The red and green jackets were small, bold squares of colour against the sky. The wind pulled at the ends of the angora scarves.

'They're not going to try and get down *there*, are they?' he asked uneasily.

'It looks like it.'

'But they can't! It's far too steep.'

'Of course they can. It isn't steep at all.'

'It looks dangerous.'

'Oh, my God!' She turned away from him, her hands clenched in her pockets.

'Well, don't be so stupid. Do you want them to kill themselves?'

'Do you *think*,' she demanded, swerving round with arms spread wide in despair, 'that I want them to kill themselves?'

'You don't exactly go out of your way to prevent it.'

Their movements on the vast, empty beach were clumsy and pointless; they blundered about as though they were blind. Laura rushed away from him, and then, without having reached any destination, stopped. Supposing it is dangerous, she thought. But it can't be. But, supposing, for once, he is right? She cupped her hands round her mouth. 'Can you get down?' she shouted cheerfully.

The two children waved, their legs dangling over the edge.

'Where's Angie?'

They pointed back along the cliff.

'Wait for her!' Geoffrey howled. 'Wait for Angie!'

The children seemed to shrug their shoulders, then slithered off the edge of the cliff and began plunging and sliding down towards the beach. They were quite safe. To them, their parents looked like two minutely circling beetles, their small fury inaudible.

'They heard me,' Geoffrey said. 'They distinctly heard me tell them to wait for Angie.'

'No. They didn't.'

'They heard me, and they blatantly disobeyed. I congratulate you, Laura. You're doing a wonderful job. Really wonderful.'

'Oh, Geoffrey ...' She felt trapped with him on the huge beach. Could it really be possible that even here, with the great light sky and the sea that stretched, she vaguely believed, to Russia, he could make her feel as though they were in a small city room – doorless, windowless, the only air the warm, wasted breath of their quarrelling? She turned as though to ask him this.

He mistook her look of despair for love, for contrition at making him so unhappy. He grabbed at her arm. 'Laura,' he said. 'Look, Laura.'

'Yes?'

'Look, I've got to go in a little while. Couldn't we ...'

'Couldn't we what?'

Her face was frozen again. She froze at the touch of his hand, but he didn't realise this. She hates me, he thought. She really hates me. But why? Why? What have I done wrong? The wind blew a heavy strand of hair across her eyes. He released her from it, gently replacing the hair, tucking it behind her ear. For the first time, he dimly realised that if she hated him, she suffered, and that what she felt was, now, perhaps unalterable. 'Come back with me,' he said.

'Why?'

'I need you.'

'What for?'

It was impossible to subdue his impatience. 'What do you mean, "What for?" Of course I need you. I can't stand living alone. You know I can't.'

'Oh,' she said. 'I see.'

She looked back towards the cliff. He realised that she was suddenly dispirited. As she dwindled inside herself into someone old and resigned and tired of fighting, he felt, unaware of the reason, a drabness in the afternoon. It was, of course, Sunday. The train would be slow. And yet when he got there, the telephone would be waiting, yesterday's letters, the bottle of Scotch he had bought last Wednesday evening. He would have the bathroom to himself and could go to sleep without apologising. It wouldn't be too bad after all.

Apologising? Good God, what had he got to apologise for?

'There's Angie,' Laura said.

The two elder children were halfway down the cliff. Angie had appeared at the top and was looking down. She succeeded, so small and motionless in her blue jacket, in storming the emptiness that her parents had failed to disturb. Her reluctance, her uncertainty and fear were so powerful that she became, without making a sound, the centre of the vast landscape. Her sisters, clinging like spiders to the soft cliff wall, craned their necks. The parents stood with their faces raised, stricken with doubt.

'She'll never make it,' Geoffrey said. 'Tell her to go back and come down the path.'

Laura said nothing.

'Will you tell her?' Geoffrey demanded. 'Will you please tell her, before she breaks her neck?'

'She'll be all right,' Laura said quietly.

'All right? Are you crazy? Can't you see she's frightened?' He began waving both arms. 'Go back!' he shouted. 'Come down by the path!'

The child did not move. Sarah and Catherine, curious at all the fuss, peered down over their shoulders. Sarah lost her grip and slithered a few feet in a flurry of sand.

'There you are!' Geoffrey screamed. 'There you are! They'll kill themselves!' He started off towards the cliff, slowly and urgently, like a man in a dream.

He mustn't do it, Laura thought. He mustn't. She meant that he mustn't make them mean and timid, that he must allow his children to be brave and not imprison them in the small room, the cosy cell in which they, the parents, inched through their narrow lives. All this was not considered but sprung violently out of her as she watched the paunchy city man struggling across the sand, the wind flattening the neat creases of his trousers.

'Don't!' she shouted. 'Geoffrey! Don't!' She began to run.

As she caught up with him, he shouted, 'You're crazy!' foolishly wasting his breath, pounding on.

'Leave her alone, Geoffrey! Please!'

'Why?'

'Let her try,' she implored. 'At least let her try!'

He stopped, making a megaphone of his hands. 'Go back!' he yelled. 'You can't do it, Angie! Go back!'

The child sat down on the brink of the cliff.

Laura stood still. She stared up at the child. Go on, she urged her soundlessly. Go on, Angie. You can do it.

'Stop her!' Geoffrey was shouting, signalling wildly to Sarah and Catherine high above him. 'Stop her!'

Go on, Laura insisted with tenderness. Please, Angie. Jump.

With sudden decision, the child jumped, tumbling and scrabbling down the sandy wall until she found a foothold. Then, rather shakily, she stood and began to pick her way down. Geoffrey, who had reached the bottom of the cliff, made a few ineffectual attempts to pull himself up by the insecure scrub. Laura could hear him railing furiously against Sarah and Catherine. Lolling above him on a hump of grass, they seemed to look at him sympathetically but without much interest. Accepting at last that Angie was far enough down to be safe, he gave up. He stood beating the sand off his suit, shaking it out of the cuffs of his trousers. Then, with furious dignity, he walked over to Laura.

She was smiling, hugging her coat round her hips. 'Well,' she said. 'She did it. I told you so.'

'All right,' he said testily. 'Angie climbed down a cliff. What does that prove?'

'Prove?' Do you really mean, her look asked, that you don't know?

'Yes,' he insisted savagely. 'Yes. What does it prove? That you encourage your children to break their necks, that's what it proves. For nothing. Teaching them to be bloody melodramatic show-offs like yourself.'

'Oh,' she said. She looked vaguely away. The wind whipped her hair across her face again, and she pushed it back, as though this, and nothing else, troubled her. 'Is that what you think?'

'Why *can't* you be reasonable?' he demanded.

'I'm sorry,' she said lightly. She was watching Angie, certain now, running down the cliff as though it were a staircase.

'Why don't you come back to London, so that we can live an ordinary, sensible life?'

'Because we've taken a house here,' she said absently. 'Because it's the holidays and the summer, and the children like it. Because . . .'

'All right,' he snapped. 'All right. I know all that, for God's sake.'

'Well, then,' she said softly, as though dismissing him, as though this were all.

They began walking slowly back towards the path. Sarah and Catherine were climbing down from their perch. In a few moments they would be on the beach, and whatever anguish, whatever frustration had been hinted at, would again be left unresolved. A tremendous reluctance dragged at Geoffrey's feet, weighed down his shoulders. 'It's this blasted place,' he said. 'It wasn't like this before.'

'Before when?'

'The other summers you've been away.'

'It was always like this before. We were younger, that's all.'

He stopped, stamping his foot in fury. It was like slamming a swing door; the wet sand made no sound, even his footprint immediately disappeared.

'Why, *why* will you dramatise everything? Of course we weren't younger. What the hell do you mean?'

'Last year,' she said, 'I should have thought we were younger. Angie was only six. I remember. You wouldn't let her ride on a donkey, in case she fell off.' She looked up at him sidewise, coldly, without smiling.

'A year doesn't make all that difference. You're sending me back to London without one sign of affection, do you realise that? Without one civil word? Simply because I'd sooner have my children alive than dead. Simply because I want a sensible, ordinary life instead of all this . . .' He swept around at the sea, the placid beach, the soft, harmless cliffs; he took in the children, balancing on the edge of the last eight-foot drop, and returned the angry, boomerang glance to his wife. She met his stare calmly, knowing what he saw.

'This what?' she asked. Her pale lips were dried by the sea air; her body, inside the heavy, almost armoured clothes, was cramped with disuse. She lived in her clothes in restricted, solitary confinement. 'Well?' She repeated patiently, 'This what?'

'Hooliganism,' he said, as though the curious word had been made for him at that moment. 'Ridiculous hooliganism.'

A thin cheer came from the cliff. They turned and saw Angie edging herself down the last few feet. Sarah and Catherine were already on the beach. They stood with straddled legs, the seats of their jeans baboon-orange from the sand.

'Jolly good!' they shouted, in their precise, cultured voices. 'Jolly good, Angie!'

'Well,' Geoffrey mumbled. 'I must go. I don't suppose I need bother to say goodbye. They won't notice the difference. Goodbye, Laura.'

'Of course you must say goodbye.' She took his arm, as though he were a shy guest at a cocktail party. When he's gone, she thought, I can climb the cliff, too. 'Of course you must say goodbye,' she repeated, suddenly gushing.

'Well.' He raised his voice in a dismal shout. 'Goodbye, everyone! See you on Friday!'

Sarah and Catherine turned and waved. Angie turned and waved. There was a small explosion of sand, the flash of a blue jacket, then – while the smiles still hung on their faces – scream after scream, the child writhing and arching herself at the bottom of the cliff, a few clods of sand falling after her in a dwarf landslide.

They both ran towards her. A tuft of grass she had been clinging to had given way; she was still holding a fistful of it. She had fallen perhaps four feet, hardly more than her own height.

'She fell,' Sarah said anxiously. 'Just that little way. She fell.'

'Of course she fell!' Geoffrey wailed. 'Of course she did!' He knelt down and tried to take the child in his arms. She screamed terribly, twisting away from him.

'It's her leg,' Catherine said excitedly. 'Look, it's her leg!'

The child's jeans had wrinkled up to her knees. Laura, kneeling beside Geoffrey, saw the shin-bone sticking up like a piece of snapped celery under the taut, sandy skin.

'I think it's broken,' she said dully. 'Geoffrey. I think it's broken.'

For a moment he turned and looked at her. His face was grey with distress, but his eyes – the tired, disappointed eyes – were shining. They were lit with triumph. He's glad, she thought incredulously. He doesn't know it, but he is actually glad.

'I told you she'd fall,' he said quietly. 'I told you so.'

He gathered up the child and, without waiting for Laura, Sarah or Catherine, began climbing very slowly, very carefully up the cliff path. His shoes slipped from time to time on the concrete. He tested every step before relying on it. He did not attempt to comfort the child. He allowed her to cry, carrying her with great pride and caution, as though she were a treasure he had won, a rare and valuable hostage.

LITTLE MRS PERKINS

y third child was born in a vast maternity hospital in South London. For the first two days, I shared a room in the private wing of this hospital with a Mrs Isaacs, but on the day after my daughter's birth, Mrs Isaacs returned home. Although we had, in a way, lived in the greatest intimacy during this time, we were by no means friendly. In fact, we had hardly spoken to each other until her departure except to mumble a faint hallo as she pattered briskly past the end of my bed in her high-heeled mules and candlewick dressing gown, always clutching great tins and bags of toilet requisites (I'm sure this is what she called them), as though setting off on a picnic. For two days, on the other side of the blue curtain that divided the room into cubicles, I had listened to her telephone conversations and endured hours of uncertainty over the name of her new child. '. . . Well, I don't know, dear. Allen likes "Lisa", but Mother seems set on "Carolyn" . . . Well, it's not as though it was really in the family, you know what I mean . . . Well, Grandma's name – that's Ruth. Yes, it's a pretty name, but I don't feel it suits her. Oh, she's ever so cute – blue eyes . . . Yes, I *know* they all have blue eyes . . .' I had nothing against Mrs Isaacs, but when I heard her packing that Wednesday afternoon I was very relieved.

As she left, her neatly suited, plump husband beaming over his load of bags and baskets, she paused for a moment by the cot at the end of my bed. The babies were brought round for feeding, and it was usually an hour or so before they were taken back to the nursery. 'Congratulations,' she said. 'Boy or girl?'

'Girl.'

'What are you going to call her?'

I said I had no idea.

'Oh. Well. Bye-bye, then. Best of luck.'

'Thank you,' I said. 'Same to you.'

When she had gone, I enjoyed, for a few minutes, the feeling of ownership. The telephone was mine, the room was mine; with any luck, they would move me over into Mrs Isaac's bed, with its uninterrupted view of the suburban street. Mrs Isaac's flowers – carnations and maiden fern – were turning brown in their cut-glass vases. Mrs Isaac's magazines, each with a good long chunk of serial and a superior knitting pattern, were neatly piled on her locker. I fell asleep.

The nurses attacking Mrs Isaac's half of the room did not, for some reason, disturb me. When I awoke, the flowers and magazines were gone, the bed chaste as a marble slab, the dividing curtains drawn back, so that I felt for the first time a cool, withdrawing finger of sunlight and saw the trolley buses moving like launches up and down the misty street. My daughter had been taken away, and, suddenly drained of all my enthusiasm for being alone, I rang the bell. The red light glared over the door; faint, muffled, the squawk of a hundred babies sounded down the hall, unmelodious as a chicken farm at dawn; but nobody came. I telephoned home, but there was no answer – my mother must be marching the children round the park. I telephoned my husband, but he was out. I wept, as much for the occupation as anything else. I thought longingly of Mrs Isaacs, who had exerted the stabilising, depressing influence of home.

The double doors opened at last, but not for me. Through them, with some caution, nosed the front of a trolley; it stopped midway while a muttered conversation went on outside. I saw the head and shoulders of a young woman – spikes of blonde hair awry on the pillow and a pink face so blotched and swollen with grief that it seemed formless as a child's; the rest of her, as she finally coasted into the room, was covered with a sheet. Briskly, without a glance at me, the nurses who followed drew the dividing curtain. Through the door, diffidently half in, half out, miserably peering for signs of the vanished trolley, came a young man clasping a number of loose objects – cosy pink schoolgirl's slippers, trousseau dressing-gown, sponge bag, rolled umbrella. His long, schoolboy face, topped with plastered hair, was indescribably wretched. 'Good afternoon,' he muttered – polite (he would always be polite), hurried from some office, Foreign, Home, Colonial, and involved, on a Wednesday afternoon, in something beyond him.

'In here, Mr Perkins,' the nurse corrected him. Blushing, he struggled through the curtain, and I heard several sounds – the umbrella dropping, Mr Perkins becoming entangled in something, apologising, the little sobs of his wife like a distraught child's. Then the nurses raced past the end of my bed and out of the door with the empty trolley. The three of us, the Perkinses and myself, were briefly alone.

I could not see them, of course. I lay stiff, hiding in my bed, for fear of embarrassing them.

The girl cried.

'It'll be all right, darling,' Mr Perkins whispered urgently. 'Everything's going to be all right . . .'

She cried.

'It'll be all right, darling, honestly, I promise you.'

She cried still more.

The staff nurse swooped through the doors and said almost tenderly, 'Now, Mr Perkins, if you would care to wait outside . . .'

'Of course,' he muttered but did not, from the sound of it, move. A ditherer, crushed between authority and longing, he would never make up his mind. His wife's puffed eyes would keep him, the nurse's tender bark send him away; so he would fidget, and do nothing. I lit a cigarette with the same feeling of worldliness that I had felt at fourteen. The cigarette had the same taste, and I stifled a fit of coughing.

'*Please!*' the nurse said, darting an angry head through the curtain, then withdrawing. 'Wait outside, Mr Perkins,' she snapped. Almost immediately, he stumbled past the foot of my bed, nodding again in the general direction of my agonised smile, my breath held to bursting, my tear-filled eyes. I imagined him sitting outside, alone, shuddering at the remote autumnal smell of anaesthetic.

'Nurse,' I said. 'Isn't it six o'clock?' I knew it was six o'clock, but the place had made me cowardly.

'Please!' Her indrawn breath whispered. The curtain swung back into stillness.

'So they can all starve,' I said. 'All your bonny, hygienically delivered, £100-a-time babies can starve, I suppose.' But I was careful to say this only with my lips, making no sound.

On the other side of the curtains, forms were being filled in. Whatever the pain, hope or despair, a catalogue must be made: Pamela Amanda Perkins, aged twenty-four; living in Westminster; husband's full name David Alexander

Perkins, profession independent theatrical manager (I had been wrong there); no previous confinements; no illnesses – but yes, how stupid, she'd forgotten scarlet fever at school; no operations, unless you count tonsils when she was five. What was wrong with her, then, I asked myself; why the misery? A strong, healthy girl finely dusted with baby powder and the possessor, no doubt, of a string of twenty-one choice pearls and a few small diamonds. Why, for God's sake, all this fuss? Tomorrow she'd be wrapped in angora and the flowers would be climbing up the walls and David Alexander putting down the port. I allowed myself an exasperated groan.

'Now try to relax, dear,' the nurse was saying.

'But I want to *keep* . . .' The rest was lost in a wail.

'I know, dear. I'll send you a little pill.'

It was not for another hour that I discovered that little Mrs Perkins – it was odd how quickly, in my mind, she changed her stature – was not in fact having a baby at all, but trying desperately to save one. The babies had been brought round at last; her doctor had come. Her doctor, a Mr Macaulay, was better dressed, slightly more suntanned than mine; otherwise, like all successful obstetricians, he looked like a one-time matinée idol who, in early middle age, had struck oil. 'Now, Mrs Perkins.' I could hear the click of his smile, radiating warmth. 'What's all this? What's all this, eh? A little pain? You tell me where.'

She murmured something.

He was not, I felt, listening to her. 'We'd better have a look at you. You won't mind a spot of anaesthetic?'

I didn't hear her answer. My daughter, in her cot at the foot of my bed, began to cry. Mr Macaulay came through the curtain, took hold of the cot, and guided it expertly out of the door.

'Sorry,' he said, when he came back. Then, as a vague afterthought, 'Hope you don't mind.'

'Not a bit,' I said, knowing it made no difference.

Mrs Perkins was sobbing again.

'Tears won't help,' Mr Macaulay said. 'You've got to be a good, brave girl. No one's going to hurt you. We're all on your side.' He made these remarks absently, patting her with words.

'But is there any *hope*?'

'Of course there's hope. You've probably been gadding about too much, that's all. Some can, some can't – that's old Mother Nature for you. Just try to relax.'

'I will,' she whispered. 'I will, honestly.'

After that, she was very quiet. I could feel her, beyond the curtain, trying to relax. The nurses came and went, making a kind of clumsy effort to be gentle. I longed to say something encouraging to her. I shared her dread. When my husband came to see me, I made him whisper, and he left after a quarter of an hour. At last they came and wheeled Mrs Perkins, fast asleep, away.

I didn't hear them bring her back. I woke, as usual, to a stout cup of tea at half past five in the morning and the cacophony of hungry children. There was no sound from Mrs Perkins. With remarkable mercy, they let her sleep. The day crept on, minute by attenuated minute. A West Indian with beautiful earrings came and polished the floor, an old woman delivered the newspapers, the matron appeared and told me that she had seen a very nice picture with Deborah Kerr but couldn't remember its name. I longed to ask someone about Mrs Perkins, but knew that no one would tell me if I did.

At last, around eleven, she stirred. The nurses immediately began badgering her. 'Well, you *have* had a nice sleep, dear, your husband phoned, he's coming this afternoon . . . UPsy daisy, OVER you go.' I heard nothing from her but little sounds that might have been gratitude or protest; they were no longer, thank goodness, sad. When the nurses finally left her alone, I found I could make out through the curtain the flat, still shape of her bed, and I could hear her breathing. The sunlight, cold outside but warm through the closed window, was growing stronger. We lay silent in the tart smell of floor polish – drowsy, strangers to each other, but both, for the moment at least, peaceful.

Mr Macaulay arrived about midday. He was wearing a beautiful dark grey overcoat and a silk muffler. He nodded to me kindly as he passed my bed, and the peace was destroyed. He was quite right, of course, to have given orders not to allow my daughter in the room except for feeding, but on the other hand he might, considering me deprived, pause, give me the benefit of his opinion on the weather – even, perhaps, ask after my health. My own doctor, having announced that there was nothing more he could do for me except send in the bill, had gone to Majorca. I was now in the charge of a house doctor much too busy for casual visiting, and I was lonely.

For the first time, I heard Mrs Perkins speaking in what I thought must be her normal voice. It was a high, very young voice; perhaps at finishing school she had taken elocution classes against the day when she would have to launch a liner or open a church bazaar. 'Am I all right?' she asked eagerly. 'Is everything all right? I feel *madly* well.'

'Of course you're all right,' Mr Macaulay assured her. 'You've just got to take it easy, that's all. No antics.'

'Antics?'

'Dancing, riding – whatever it is you do, dashing about on those murderous high heels.'

'Oh.' She breathed a little laugh, as though telling him not to be ridiculous. 'Oh, I see. That's wonderful. That's really *wonderful*.'

'I mean it. Mornings in bed. Asleep by ten every night. You've got help?'

'Oh yes, nanny . . .'

'Good. Then take it easy. I don't guarantee anything; you never can in this business. But if you do what you're told and sit tight, the chances are very good. Do you knit?'

'No.'

'Paint? Read? Sew? Anything like that?'

'Well, no.'

'Then now's the time to start. You'd better stay here for a couple of days, so we can keep an eye on you. And you're to call me at the first sign of a pain – you promise me that?'

'Pain?' She didn't understand the word. 'But that won't be till . . .?'

'We hope not.'

You fool, I thought, why can't you trust her? Can't you see how much she wants this child? It's all going to be all right, I wanted to shout, and you'll have a splendid picture in the *Queen*, and your own darling nanny to feed it on Robinson's Groats, just like she fed you; and the high grey pram will be seen in the park, and in the summer its canopy will give green shade from the common sun; and David will cry by the telephone before he sits down to write the announcement for *The Times*. It's all going to be all right. Why can't the man tell her?

'The chances are very good indeed,' he said. 'It all depends on you.'

'Yes,' she said humbly.

'I'll have a word with your husband, tell him to cosset you.'

'Oh, we're going to Tenerife next week – Mummy's taken a house there – so I'll be *madly* cosseted.' She had revived, was smiling again.

Mr Macaulay hesitated for a fraction of a second. If I could have seen him, I doubt whether I would have noticed it. Then he said smoothly, 'Very nice. I wish I could do the same.'

He left. The silver autumn sunlight filled Mrs Perkins's half of the room, and when lunch came I saw a sharper silhouette through the blue curtain, eating, the plate under her chin, with quick, dainty mouthfuls. I felt guilty to be watching her without speaking. On the other hand, she knew by now that I was there. She could talk if she wanted to. Had she no friends, relatives whom she wanted to telephone? Apparently not. After lunch, she settled down and, as far as I could tell, fell into a sound sleep.

I had almost forgotten what she looked like. Her problem, I felt sure, was solved. They left my daughter in her cot at the end of my bed, and she, too, was quiet. The three of us breathed secretly, like children in dormitories pretending to be dead.

It was mid-afternoon when Mr Perkins came to see his wife. Without knowing it, I had slept. A quick look and a strong smell of perfume assured me that Mrs Perkins was well on the road to recovery. The shadow, against orders, was sitting up; she probably had bows in her hair.

'Darling . . .' they both said, and there was silence.

'How is it?' he asked. 'How do you feel? They said you were—'

'Marvellous. Hush – that woman's asleep.'

'My poor darling. My poor, brave darling.' He actually said these words.

'But anyway,' she said, 'it's all right now. You know, it was awful, but all the time I was thinking what a *waste*—'

'No, you mustn't . . .'

'I mean, whether I could sell all those madly pricy clothes, and what a good thing we only paid a deposit on the pram.'

'No, no,' he said. 'It wouldn't have mattered.'

'And I'm so relieved. So glad – are you glad?'

This last question was so gentle, so much requiring a gesture of love, that I was ashamed. They were silent for a few moments. I did not look at the curtain. His answer, obviously, had been given.

She burst out again. 'And now we can whiz off to Tenerife and lie in the sun and forget the whole thing. Isn't it bliss?'

'You look frightfully sweet.'

'I tell you what I want you to do. There won't be much time for shopping, and anyway I'm not supposed to. Well, anyway, I've made this list.'

'Darling.'

'I haven't got a thing, you see, because I was going to pop into Treasure Cot and do it all this week. So what you've got to do is give this list to nanny. Are you listening?'

'Darling, I . . .' I looked now at the curtain. There were two distinct shadows, one sitting very upright, withdrawn towards the end of the bed. I listened intently. Something was happening. David Alexander Perkins, in agony, was trying to make a statement, but it was I, not his wife, who recognised the sounds, the attitude of strain.

'Do look, David, it's terribly important. *This* is the list for nanny, and *this* . . .'

'I had a talk with Macaulay.'

'Yes?' She faltered. The holding of her breath for that split second made an unbearable silence. 'What – what did he say?'

'That – that he didn't think it's advisable . . . I mean, if we want everything to be all right until March – and we *do*, don't we, my God, we *do?* Well, he said . . .'

'We can't go. I can't go and see Mummy.' She repeated it in a very quiet, matter-of-fact tone.

'I'm afraid not. Oh, darling, I'm dreadfully sorry.'

'He didn't say that to me.' She had a different voice now – flat, loud, almost brutal. 'I told him we were going to Tenerife. He didn't say that to me.'

'I know. He thought . . .' The absurdity of this seemed to choke him. 'He thought it would come better from me, that I should be able to . . .'

There was a long silence. They seemed paralysed. Then, thank God, her words came gently. 'I'm sorry, David. I do see. Of course I do. I'm terribly sorry.'

'*Sorry?*' His voice broke like a boy's. 'You're sorry? My God, it's me who should be sorry! All this beastly business and you're so sweet and brave, and what the hell do *I* do?'

'Hush,' she said.

'Anyway, it would have been pretty wretched for you – not being able to swim, or dance, and all that.'

'Yes,' she said. 'It would.'

'And then the journey.'

'Yes, of course.'

'I know how much you wanted to go. Perhaps your mother could come over and stay? We could easily put her up . . .'

'That's terribly sweet of you, David.'

'You see, it's just any sort of exertion might just start everything . . . Well, and then miles away from Macaulay. You do *see?* You aren't too dreadfully upset?'

'No.' It was a brave little whisper. 'Honestly I'm not. Anyway . . .' She even tried to laugh, and I was savage with myself then, for ever feeling patronising towards her. 'Anyway, you never wanted to go much, did you?'

'Don't talk like that. Please. I'd go anywhere, *anywhere* to make you happy. It was only this wretched play opening and everyone being so . . .'

'I know you felt you oughtn't to be away. Well, now you won't be. So that's something good.'

'And the baby.'

'Oh yes. Of course. The baby.'

'Perhaps it might make you feel better about Tenerife. If we lost the baby, I . . .'

'What, David?'

'I'd be dreadfully unhappy. I'm sorry.'

'Do stop being so sorry,' she said sweetly, with wonderful composure. 'It's not *your* fault we can't go . . . But perhaps I'm a bit tired. Perhaps I should rest now.'

'Of course,' he said eagerly. 'Of course you must.' After awhile, he managed to tear himself away. As he stumbled past the end of my bed, he did not look so much distressed as strengthened, almost ennobled, by relief. He even glanced at me as he said 'Good afternoon.' He had large, beautiful eyes, which gave his face an impression of weakness; otherwise, I realised, he was older than I had thought, and probably more capable. I was genuinely moved by the scene I had overheard. I was determined to speak to her.

But surprisingly – I don't know why, but by now I thought of Mrs Perkins as almost infallible – the moment he had gone she began to cry again, softly, but with the old despair. I was puzzled. It must be exhaustion; after all, she had had a severe fright. It might be disappointment, although surely a trip to Tenerife to see Mummy couldn't seem very important compared with keeping the child. She did not cry like someone stifling tears but like someone whose natural sound is weeping – quiet, regular, without pause. The afternoon sun was at its strongest, and I could almost see the little movements of her fingers as she turned her handkerchief inside out and inside out again.

Then, abruptly, she stopped. I thought she had fallen asleep. But slowly, cautiously, she was pushing back the blankets with her feet. Was she going to get out of bed? No, because, uncovered, she lay perfectly still. Then, very carefully, she raised one leg into the air; its shadow through the curtain was long, thin, wavering. She bent her knee, pushed the leg straight again. Afterwards, still very slowly and carefully, the other leg. She was testing some-thing – but what? One leg. Then the other leg. No noise, no unusual creaking of the bedsprings. Both legs circling, faster and faster. She was trying not to make a noise. She was bicycling.

I don't know how long little Mrs Perkins continued this silent and relentless marathon. Possibly it went on for ten minutes or a quarter of an hour. I knew, after the first moments of confusion, what she was trying to do, and it appalled me. But she did not know that I knew, and somehow this made it impossible for me to do or say anything to prevent her. I have thought about this frequently since then, wondering whether I should have spoken, called the nurses. I could have made a telephone call, wakened the baby; I could – and there is no other true basis for guilt and regret – have done *something*. It leads into all those long, inconclusive arguments about responsibility, which my husband enjoys so much: am I my brother's keeper, or do I just keep quiet? But this is not what I felt at the time. I simply felt that she did not know that I knew, and that it was impossible to tell her. The blue curtain was a fixed, insurmountable barrier dividing our two lives. I did, I said, nothing.

When the night nurses came down the hall, Mrs Perkins scrambled hastily back under the covers and lay still.

One of them came in.

'I'm *much* better, thank you,' I heard Mrs Perkins murmur.

'So we'll see you again in March, then? I'll put you down for twins, dear.'

'Oh, I do *hope* it won't be twins.'

'Is it a boy or a girl you're after?'

'I think girls are cosier . . .'

'Now, now, you just keep still. You can jump about as much as you like *next* time you come in.'

'I'm so sorry,' Mrs Perkins said meekly. 'I really must try to remember.'

I fed my daughter and asked the nurse to take her away. The room was quiet. I waited. I suppose we were both waiting. There were no more gymnastics, but something

SATURDAY LUNCH WITH THE BROWNINGS

that I can only describe as a steady flow of will-power. A woman waiting to have a child (although in Mrs Perkins's case it was a little different) can do this curious thing of filling an entire room, universe, with steady and indefatigable purpose. Perhaps men can do it, too – I have no experience of that. I only know it, or recognise it, as an audible beat, an intense effort for self-destruction, out of which, by some extraordinary inconsistency, something is created.

The beat stopped, the red light buzzed, around eight-thirty. A nurse came immediately.

'I'm terribly sorry,' Mrs Perkins murmured – and I could have sworn she was smiling. 'But I've got a little bit of a pain.'

I didn't see Mrs Perkins again for almost eight months. The staff nurse had grudgingly told me that she had been ill – very ill – after the miscarriage, and had spent the rest of her time in the hospital in the isolation wing.

'Did she get to Tenerife?' I asked.

'I can't say,' the nurse snapped. 'I'm not on post-natal, you know, Mrs Lewis.'

It was the beginning of June in the following year when I saw Mrs Perkins. I was wheeling my daughter – finally called Geraldine, after some aunt – back from the park, and the two other children were slopping along sucking their first iced lollies of the summer and grasping the pushchair with their free hands as we paused to cross the great width of the Brompton Road. Burdened with children and a basket load of shopping, I waited for the traffic as a timid sightseer might wait in a national park for a passing stampede of buffalo.

'Let's go,' my son insisted, casting himself off the pavement.

'No. Wait.' I grabbed him back, tense, thoughtless of anything but safety. It was at that moment I saw the Perkinses.

They were driving in a white sports car; I have no idea of the make, but it was long, low, and discreet. Little Mrs Perkins was at the wheel. She was wearing a pale-pink headscarf, and her face – deeply tanned, glossy, with a pale mouth – was set in a look of painful anger. Beside her sat David Alexander. He did not look angry. He looked as though he had been hired with the car but hadn't come up to expectations. To my amazement, the car stopped. Mrs Perkins waited, hands limp on the wheel.

'Come on. Come ON. Let's go.'

I was dragged off the pavement. Stately, condescending, a bus allowed us to pass. We had reached the other side. I turned, half raised my hand.

I know more about that woman, I thought, than any other person alive.

She inclined her head, briefly gracious, acknowledging my thanks for letting us cross the road. Then she was off, moving sedately east, her pink headscarf rigid, her brain nimbly dealing with the complexities of gear, brake, and steering wheel.

'Do you know that person?' The voice from below.

'No. Not really. Well, once.'

'She didn't know you.'

'No. that's right. She didn't know me.'

It was not until then that I realised that little Mrs Perkins had never seen me. She did not even know of my existence.

THE PARSON

He was a short, very heavy man – obese, although oddly thin in the face and with square hands, flat-tipped fingers, no flesh between the knuckles. A narrow, flat forehead that with the years grew higher, although he never appeared to become bald; eyebrows that jutted out enormously long, curly and wiry, and small eyes beneath all this tangle as sharp as terriers', but blue. They were never tender or glazed with sentiment.

His nose became larger and bonier as his forehead grew higher. As he grew older, as his face sank away from it, this nose was like the prow of Methodism rising out of a receding sea. The eyes might blaze, the eyebrows bristle, the forehead soar ever more lofty, but the nose was of chapel and sin. Around the bridge, it had a pinched look of virtue and condemnation.

A long upper lip, which might have been taken off a comedian; and a mouth that changed with time more than any other feature, starting off wide and broad-lipped and ending as a thin line, an opening slit for food or, almost non-existent, clamped round a cigarette.

All this head, with its contradictions and discrepancies, rode too large for the short, heavy body. His back view, in suspended grey flannels and shirt-sleeves, digging, weeding, mowing a lawn, was the rear of a squat old elephant – the same vast, solid grey folds ending in short, tubular legs, the same lumbering quality.

And yet he was deft. Until he became ill and lazy and clumsy, he could make or mend most things. He played chess in a series of vicious jabs, pouncing the pieces down grunting, puffing great blasts of smoke, and usually winning – his one intellectual achievement.

He was a clergyman for one reason only – there was nothing else he could possibly have been. As a small boy, bullied and teased by six sisters and four brothers, he sat under the nursery table chanting, 'Mama, Papa, all the children are disagreeable except me ...' God shone a compassionate eye through the silk tassels on the green serge tablecloth, disregarded the ten clever goody-goodies, and picked him out. He began preaching – a stocky, timid, bombastic little boy shouting of Hell-fire in the front parlour while his brothers sneered and his sisters tittered and his father played the harmonium. As a reward, his grandmother would give him lollipops, lovingly slipped from her tongue on to his. The only colour in the house was the white of the girls' petticoats whisking round dark corners.

He went to various schools, but he learned nothing. He was beaten, put in the attic, kept on bread and water. This made him cry, convinced him that he was a sinner, but made him even more stupid. At sixteen, hair slicked down from a centre parting, stiff-collared, in dog's-tooth check, he was taken away from school and bound as an apprentice in his father's printing firm. The other apprentices were disagreeable; he clung firmly to God and became a preacher in the local Wesleyan chapel, flaying the nodding bonnets with his great new voice, guiltily and savagely in love with a girl called Maisie. Maisie, a bobbish little rich girl of fifteen, was frightened and ran away; she never married, but for sixty years kept, transfixed, her startled giggle, her look of petrified alarm.

He might have gone on like this for some years, but his father died; the printing firm collapsed. He enrolled in a Methodist Theological College.

It was a ghastly mistake. Black-suited, forced to attend long lectures on the Roman baptismal creed, to puzzle his way through Athanasius and Marcellus and the Cappadocians, to battle with the theory of enhypostasia and Socinianism and kenosis, to listen to pale young men with clammy hands discussing Theodore of Mopsuestia and the laws of ecclesiastical polity – all this was the nearest thing to Hell he had ever known. God moved away from him and hid in a cloud of unknowing. For the first time in his life, with the agony of a child who sees his father pinching the maid's bottom, he had Doubts. He wept and prayed, but it was no good. The college expelled him for failing all his examinations. He thought, as he walked slowly away with his Gladstone bag and his Bible, of walking straight on into the placid river. Instead, he became a Unitarian.

He could preach again, and when he was preaching he could convince himself of anything. He shook his square hands, howled, and whispered; his huge, resonant voice shook the corrugated-iron roofs of dismal chapels, stroked the souls of girls in village halls. But afterwards, alone in his lodgings, he suffered. Preaching, although he worked as hard as he knew how to on his sermons, didn't take up much time. He had begun to read Nietzsche and, almost more furtively, H. G. Wells; he had heard, uneasily, of *Man and Superman*, and the phrase 'life-force' began to creep into his sermons. The idea of Life, which had nothing to do with living, had begun to take the place of God, who had shown Himself to have nothing to do with religion. 'Life is Love!' he bawled to a startled congregation. Pinch-mouthed, severely buttoning their gloves, they asked him to leave. He packed his 'Zarathustra' and went.

What to do with him now? He was twenty-eight, uneducated, unqualified, tormented by the sins he hadn't committed and unable to understand the ones he had, tremendously ambitious without the slightest talent for success, full of urges and yearnings and pains of the soul, frightening and frightened and altogether a mess. The family gave him a piece of land in the middle of Manitoba and sent him off, with a younger brother, to Canada. Perhaps, as the ship heaved off into the Liverpool fog, they thought they had seen the last of him.

He never found the piece of land. Perhaps he didn't really look. He took various trains in the hope of finding it, but always ended up sitting on his box in some desolate halt, waiting for a train to take him back to Winnipeg. After several of these excursions, he gave up and took a job in a printing firm. It was cold, barbaric. Everyone was disagreeable, and he spent hours every night reading Browning out loud to himself in order to keep his accent pure. Away from any form of organised religion, his doubts were calmed; the longer he stayed a printer, the firmer his faith became. After a year of it, he wrote home for his passage money. His cold, ink-stained fingers could hardly hold the pen. 'I know,' he wrote, 'that God intends me for the Ministry.'

His mother flew into one of her rages, whistled 'Worthy Is the Lamb' under her breath, and sent her daughters cowering to their rooms. But she was lonely. All her sons had left her and, with this one exception, were living brash and ungodly lives, both in jail and out. One was company-promoting in Sydney; another was razing Kanaka villages to the ground and living with a native girl who played the mouth organ and filled his shoes with sugar; another had just killed a lumber-man in an argument and temporarily disappeared. She sent the passage money.

So he came home, chilly, chastened, and full of hope. He would study, he would do what he was told. Somebody must want him; somebody must recognise his ability. As he set foot on English soil at Liverpool, he felt that one blast of his voice would be enough. 'Why,' bishops would ask each other, 'has he been neglected so long?'

Six months later, in a tweed hat and knickerbockers, he was bicycling about the lanes of Southern England, his heavy head bent low over the handlebars, his stout legs numbly pedalling. He was an itinerant preacher again. Browning went with him everywhere and his text was always the same: ''Tis not what man does that exalts him, but what man would do.' He read 'Saul' aloud, with great passion, in the drawing-rooms of the local gentry. One of their daughters, a handsome, strong-willed, ailing woman of thirty-five, fell in love with him. They married at eight o'clock one morning in a thick fog, walking to the chapel through muddy fields and going off to a disastrous honeymoon in lodgings at Eastbourne.

Marriage, far from calming him, goaded him to a kind of fury. He had always been violently, if furtively, conscious of sex; now, legitimately sexual, he became intoxicated with the idea that the world was more or less equally divided into men and women. Free love and the life-force and the emancipation of women all whirled together in his innocent brain, causing an extraordinary chaos in which women were exactly like men and yet were at the same time accessible. His heart gave out under the strain. He became ill. His wife had a nervous breakdown. The Wesleyans turned him out. His in-laws, stern materialists who believed devoutly in success, refused to have anything to do with him. There seemed, this time, no way out.

But, of course, there was. All his life he had been beating his head against the narrow limits of Nonconformity. The Church of England, that great, placid, unshakable compromise, loomed calm and radiant over the horizon. Why had he never thought of it before? The gracious, socially acceptable vicarages; the brown, book-lined studies where even a heretic could sleep undisturbed; the great cathedrals that could ring with his reading of Isaiah, of which he was rightly proud; and, above all, the limitless scope for a man of talent. Revived, with passionate energy and pinbright faith, he went off to Lambeth Palace and the Archbishop of Canterbury.

The first question he was asked was whether he had any money. None. Oxford or Cambridge? Neither. Who would speak for him? No one. A fortnight later, a letter came from the palace, signed with one spidery name; he was not, it was thought, suitable for the Church of England.

Now it was a case of do or die. Browning was no longer any use to him; neither was life-force. He was well into his thirties, and God was passing him by. He badgered, he pestered, he wrote long, impassioned letters. For the first time in his life he worked, swallowing great chunks of doctrine and not daring to think how uneasily it lay. The end – the study with its armchair and the mellow peal of bells – was all that mattered. When at last they accepted him, he wept for joy, although with the appearance of awful grief. Once in the Church, he knew, nothing short of murder or flagrant adultery would get him out.

They gave him the job of curate in a parish in the East End of London. His residence was a little slum house next to the gasworks; lascars prowled the streets at night and the church was a grimy great place with a sparse scattering of old women who wanted to take the weight off their feet and get away for an hour or two from their drunken husbands. He found himself looking with hostile envy at the local Catholic priest, but, of course, it was too late for that. He applied himself to the business of visiting the sick, who were very sick, and whom he found very disagreeable.

However, London had something to be said for it. He

went, having carefully removed his dog collar, to a private performance of 'Mrs Warren's Profession'; he got to know a few vaguely literary personalities – the humble outer fringe of the Café Royal world; he began to write himself, pouring out his untidy feelings on life and sex and God in dull, pompous sentences to which his wife listened with an expression of hopeless martyrdom that eventually became permanent. For her, as a curate's wife, there had begun the lifelong task of keeping up appearances; she did this with increasing skill, but once alone with her husband she became quite silent, an industrious shadow, locked and bolted against attack.

They were now secure. He was still fairly young, his great energy still untapped. The ideas pullulating inside him were still unexpressed; an East End curacy was hardly enough. He began looking around for something more alive, something with more scope.

He was offered a village that consisted of a cosy huddle of cottages under a gentle, sheltering hill. The Squire's eighteenth-century mansion faced serenely away from the church, in its wilderness of moon daisies. The vicarage stood quiet in the sun, protected by a high pink wall – a great house full of dark passages and damp stone, mellow with dust and the smell of rotting apples. There was no sound but the swing of milk pails carried on their wooden yoke, the clop of a tired horse, the hum of a fat bee in the honeysuckle. It was hard to keep awake, and a beautiful place to die in – the Church of England at its best.

He burst in like a lion, scattering teacups and raising the warm dust. For the first time in his life, he felt a sense of power. 'Yes, Vicar,' the villagers said. 'Of course, Vicar.' They pulled their forelocks, and the Squire raised his hat.

'"The voice of him that crieth in the wilderness, Prepare ye the way of the Lord, make straight in the desert a highway ..."' He was back in form again. The church shook with Isaiah, and the moon daisies were scythed down. He had a son and two hundred and fifty pounds a year, he had a study with an armchair, and six days off a week. There was only one thing missing. He no longer believed in God.

It was a terrible realisation. Not only did he not believe in God, he didn't believe in the Thirty-Nine Articles, the Virgin Birth, the idea of the Trinity, the Resurrection, the sanctity of marriage or the conception of original sin. They had all, in the security and promise of his new life, deserted him.

He began desperately to try to fill the great gap. His faith in Life became almost fanatic; loving Life and living Love – it was comprehensive, unanswerable. If anyone was foolish enough to ask him exactly what it meant, his eyes blazed more fiercely than ever, he flung his arms wide and shouted, 'You ask me what Life means? Life! Life speaks for itself!'

But he had to find some more practical expression for it. The villagers seemed smugly content with their uninspired existence, and those whom he buried were undeniably dead. He persuaded the Squire that what was needed was a village club, a place where they could come together as a community and live a little. He helped to build it, slapping on the cement – braces straining over his great shoulders – singing at the top of his voice. It was a very ugly building, a gabled and stuccoed monstrosity among the thatched cottages and rosy brick, but when it was finished the villagers obediently used it, playing slow games of billiards and watching with delight the children of the local gentry making fools of themselves on the over-elaborate stage. It was finished, and a great hopelessness came over him as he looked at it, a great hatred of his parishioners who shambled about its clean and empty rooms. It was not enough and they were not enough. There must be something more – but what?

He was now forty-six and his wife was over fifty. His son had been followed, painfully, after five intervening years, by a daughter. He took to spending most of the milder days in a summer-house at the bottom of the garden. He began sleeping in the afternoons, waking with a start to a black world of sin and atonement, the ghostly roaring of his own voice. But the sun poured lazily down through the apple trees and there was nothing to do – hours and days of nothing to do. He had a few weeks of keeping hens, who were given incredible incubators and runs of revolutionary design. One by one, they died. Two savage dogs, whom he christened Loyalty and Verity, took over the runs. They devoured the drawing-room curtains while everyone was in church, and shortly afterwards the runs were empty. Their enormous collars, together with their leads and a whistle on a leather thong, hung about for some time and then were thrown by children into the tall nettles.

He still filled the church with his voice, bellowing at the deaf Squire and the old women, who had heard him a thousand times, but it was becoming an effort. He would often break off after five minutes, abruptly mutter the names of the Father, Son, and Holy Ghost, and stamp out of the pulpit. The sense of futility made him physically ill. Unable to deafen himself with ideas, he had begun to listen to the ticking of the clock, the almost inaudible snapping of decay. There was still, perhaps, time to get out.

But, of course, he couldn't get out. The Church had him trapped as effectively as if he were behind bars. He exchanged his village for an amorphous jumble of suburban streets with identical houses crammed with office girls and bank clerks. The vicarage overlooked the railway line and shuddered all night with the crash and scream of shunting trucks. He started a youth club and preached his splendid, meaningless sermons to huge congregations of children – fifteen-year-old girls, who loved him, and adolescent boys with nothing better to do. 'Life!' he shouted at them desperately. 'Believe in Life!' He grasped the edge of the pulpit, the tears ran down his face, he laughed, he flung his spectacles into the congregation, narrowly missing his wife, who was sitting, suffering tortures of embarrassment and misery, in the front pew. When it was all over, he would go home and play the piano – loud, frustrated, unskilful chords – or shut himself in his study and sit doing nothing until, mercifully, he fell asleep.

He began toying with theosophy, anthroposophy, spiritualism. His wife, perhaps out of loneliness, had always had a very reasonable relationship with ghosts, and this, at least – the need for something mysterious in a life spent cutting up small pieces of bread for Communion, or carrying cans of water from the kitchen tap to the font or footing the bill for sacramental wine – they had in common. For a short while, it drew them together, but whereas she was content not to believe very much, his craving for belief grew greater as the possibility of satisfying it grew less. He could by now believe ten contradictory theories at the same time, and they tossed around in his soul like dead leaves, never settling, useless, whispering in the emptiness. The day he discovered Communism, he believed, with great gratitude, that he was saved.

Once again his energy soared. Reckless, enthusiastic, he devoted a whole issue of the parish magazine to supporting the Soviet persecution of the Church. Christ, he argued, was a Communist anyway. Nobody understood it. He was amazed. At last, after so much searching, he believed he had found the true meaning of Christianity. Did the Church of England not care for Christianity?

Apparently it didn't. He was advised to go north, where, it was hoped, he might sink into oblivion.

The square, gloomy house rose like a fortress out of a forest of dripping shrubs – laurel and rhododendron, privet and yew. The cotton mills and foundries glowed like Hell under a steel sky, and the huge church, built in memory of the Napoleonic Wars, echoed like a tomb for the few living souls who crept inside it.

Wearily, with the resignation of a man who has been through this move many times before, he started a youth club. He was over fifty – the prime, he insisted aggressively, of life – and so heavy that it became increasingly difficult for him to move about. He went everywhere by car, hunched over the wheel, saluting his parishioners with a gesture that was half gracious, half insulting. For days at a time, he sat in his study – the same desk, the same armchair, the same glass-fronted bookshelves – speaking to no one, scribbling away at some new work that was to enlighten the world, or trying to crowd out the emptiness with bits of Bertrand Russell, a few predigested scraps of Einstein, populating his desert with Ethel Mannin, A. S. Neill, Rudolf Steiner, Mme Blavatsky, Krafft-Ebing. Every Saturday, in a hushed house, he wrote what he thought was a new sermon, but they were all the same, a torment of words disgorged to a slowly dwindling congregation. His voice was still remarkable, but it had nothing to say. He longed for the existence of someone to whom he could say he was sorry. There was no one. For the first time in over twenty years, he brought the photograph of his mother out of his drawer, and set it between his watch and his collar box on the bedroom mantelpiece.

One day, while conducting a funeral service, he stumbled and fell into the open grave. Climbing out, cumbersome and horrified and ashamed, his surplice streaked with mud, he knew that everything was really over. He was not even afraid of death. It was no more than a hole in the ground, a box in the earth. He apologised, finished the service, and went home. There was nothing else he could do.

His searching now had the desperation of a man finally cornered, without sanctuary. He became a nudist. But there was nothing among the dripping trees but a group of elderly ladies dressed in spectacles, knitting scarves for their less enlightened relatives. At this time, he weighed over sixteen stone, and there was much of him to suffer. He spent one wretched night in the chalet he had booked for three weeks, and came home. The next morning, as dawn burst over the cotton mills, he was to be seen wandering naked about the shrubbery, a great, pale, disconsolate shape in the gritty light, looking for something irretrievably lost.

At the age of sixty, already an old man, he drifted west, setting up his desk, his armchair, his bookshelves in yet another study, laboriously climbing the stairs of a new

pulpit, looking down from it on the same faces, the same
bowed heads, the same expressions of patient boredom.
The Church of England had fulfilled its promise; he was
still alive, his children had been educated, he was sure of
a pension, however small. With a sort of awkward gratitude, he tried to do his best. He started a youth club. He
introduced religious film shows into the church. Some
forgotten superstition, stirring again at last, prevented
him from putting the screen on the altar, which, since
the church was small, was the obvious place. He fixed it
up between the choir stalls, and the congregation peered
intently, uncomprehending, at the vast shadows, vaguely
Oriental in appearance, that flickered, unfocused, between
the damp Norman pillars. The electrical part of the appa-
ratus was unreliable, and to prevent himself from getting
severe shocks he wore thick crêpe-soled shoes under his
surplice. But the films disgusted him. He gave them up, and
the congregation, temporarily doubled, died away. He sat
longer and longer in his study, the room thick with smoke,
Elgar or Sibelius blaring from the record-player, a novel
from the local library propped inside a mildewed tome on
psychology or ethics. He gave up writing, gave up sending
his manuscripts away. He gave up composing sermons
and extemporised, meandering on about Life while the
children fidgeted and the two old women yawned behind
gloved hands and his wife, now years younger than he,
thought briskly about something else.

Sometimes, like a man stirring in his sleep, he began to think that he must move, must change, must get out of it all. But the thought was never finished. His eyes closed, Sibelius played on unheeded, soft mounds of ash fell on his darned grey pullover. When he woke, it was time for another meal. In silence, they ate scantily, shovelling in the careless food. The house crumbled and peeled round them, unmended, uncared for. He gave up having his daily bath, came down from his cold, ascetic bedroom at the top of the house to the luxurious spare room, with its great mahogany furniture and brass fire-irons and little pots of dried lavender. An old, sick clergyman, he would have done better to die and be buried with honour and a rural dean in attendance. Instead, for the last time, the removal van came and took away the desk, the armchair, the book-shelves. The Church thanked him and sent him out into the world with six pounds a week and a few cordial letters of good wishes. For the first time in fifty years, Sunday became a day like any other.

He sat in a ground-floor room in North London; the room faced south and the identical rooms opposite, the identical front gardens with neat little curly girls in white socks carefully riding their tricycles on the paths. For over a year, the old man sat at his desk in this room, with the city sun pouring through the William Morris curtains.

God knows what passed through his mind. Meals came and were eaten. He was pitifully hungry, but they said he must lose weight – dandelion coffee and starch-reduced rolls – and he was beyond complaining. The days merged into months, interrupted only by the absurd celebration of sleep, when he went from the desk to the bed and sat upright, differently dressed, observing darkness.

Finally, without knowing it, he died. The nurse, to whom he was just a dead old man, bustled through her routine and left him tidy, unpillowed, slightly askew on the bed. The sun poured on through the faded linen, slanted over the leather-topped desk, with its little brass name-plate, the useless books.

The letters of condolence began to arrive. 'He is passing,' they said, 'through the Gateway to a far, far greater happiness in that Glorious Kingdom beyond . . . truly thankful that his sufferings are over and now he knows, and has found what he longed for . . . Perhaps he is happier now . . . It will be a relief not to have to feel sorry for him any more, for now he has found Truth . . .' There was no confirmation and no denial. Already he existed only as a set of ideas, shifting and fading. They could do what they liked with him. There was no way in which he could speak for himself.

THE MAN WHO
LOVED PARTIES

Edward Knight sat in his swivel chair and peered upwards through the November fog at the remote Regency ceiling of his office. Fronds of gloom appeared to him to hang from the cornice. Great mucky webs of despair sagged between the brass chains of the chandelier. He took a deep breath and closed his eyes. I am six years older, he told himself, than Byron was when he died. All his youth he had assumed that he would die tragically in an unbuttoned shirt at the age of thirty-six, but his final glorious hour had receded into the past along with a few ornamental love affairs, most of his hair, and his hopes. At forty-two he was still successfully alive. God help me, he thought. It is all a hollow sham.

He waited, chins on his chest, eyes now glazed behind rimless glasses. He knew his depressions well, and this was usually the limit of them. Having faced facts, he would cautiously begin to revive.

But not this morning. This morning he was going under for the third time. He was the boy Edward, lonely as the only child in the world; the growing Edward, upset. He struggled a little, clung to ukeleles and rag-time, was scorched with a painful ambition to soft-shoe-shuffle and offer fringed girls Balkan Sobranies from a slim gold case.

His cheeks twitched. He was Byron, and burst into delayed acne. The worry of it all. He was feverish and thin. The time was never good enough; the good time could always be better. How could one tell what one was missing in the scant, necessary hours of sleep?

Would he find his feet? Yes, he would. They carried him, in fact, through the lofty doors of the Ministry of Information, and into his Golden Age. Almost twenty years later he sighed his relief and a small, sick smile – sick with longing – glowed on his desperate face.

What a party. What a wonderful party. Remember the square-shouldered girls with their great thick shoes, and hair falling over one eye? Remember their big bright mouths and their belts and their boots? The married ones expected you to look after their children if you stayed the night. And they were mostly, in those days, married.

Not Cecily, of course. His smile faded. There she was, twenty-two, a generous, untidy girl, always singing. What an occupation she was going to be; what an insurance. He longed for the scenes, the reconciliations, the daily discussions in hot rooms where yesterday was never cleared away. 'After all, dear boy, we're rational people ...' He longed for the untrustworthy friends who would jump at his tread on the stairs. 'I don't blame you, dear boy. Don't think I blame you. Let's face it, we are civilised ...' And then – his face grew cunning – one would make him cook the breakfast, and relieve him of his personal points.

The wedding party lasted for eight hours, and towards the end of it Cecily became pregnant. When he got up in the morning she had already washed the glasses. Nobody had slept on the sofa. She had even scrubbed the bathroom floor. He knew this was the end, because memory finished there. The bright light poured in, his eyelids flickered. The rest was like a rewinding film – meaningless.

Edward groaned aloud. If once more, just once more, I could live again. Once more to sleep on somebody else's sofa, shave with somebody else's razor, cook breakfast for somebody else's wife ... once more to be young. Is it all over? Must it be over? Am I extinct, a dodo at forty-two?

He spun his chair savagely, leapt away from it and landed in front of the mantelpiece. He glared at a photograph of his daughter crossing St Mark's Square – serene as always, not vulgarly stepping it but poised, as though blown by a gentle wind. I'll ring her up, he thought. Take her out. He had a split-second vision of himself, dimly lit, lowering a spoonful of brown sugar into a cupful of foam. He dropped his forehead on to the cold mantelpiece, displacing the invitations to literary luncheons, cocktails and ceremonies. No, no, he told himself. Not that. I am still too young.

'Mr Parker is here,' his secretary said, her head round the door, searching about for him. 'Ah, there you are. I thought I didn't see you go out. Mr Parker is here.'

He stood up, staggering a little.

'Who?'

'Mr Parker. Thess Parker.'

It was a difficult readjustment, but he made it. He even became old for his age.

'Who the bloody hell is Thess Parker?'

She winced slightly, turning the other cheek. She was a church-goer. She was elegant, too. She brought the parish magazine to the office and read it over coffee. St Barnabas, South Harrow. He had seen it.

'*The Lilac Moon*, Mr Knight. You think it is a remarkable achievement. For a first novel, of course.' She was using her Bo-Peep voice. She prayed continually for his return to the fold. A secretary, she had been told at her commercial school, can be a great force for good.

'He's here?'

'He's waiting.'

There was a prolonged, muffled titter from the outer office.

'In there?'

She gave a quick nod, turning about, not certain in which room she was needed most.

'What's he doing?'

'He carries' – she hesitated, and was momentarily confused – 'adhesive darts.'

He felt a small tremor of anticipation. 'What do they stick to?'

She touched her forehead with the back of her hand; her simple gold bracelet slid down and nestled in the fold of her arm. 'Anything,' she said.

There was a stifled scream.

'I think I should—'

'Send him in,' Edward said.

'Yes, Mr Knight.'

'And switch on the light. I can't see a damned thing.'

'Yes, Mr Knight.'

The fog was thickening. In the discreet light of the stand-ard lamp Mr Parker advanced surrounded by a wavering nimbus, as though from another world. Edward took the strong, hot hand. He saw the filthy, belted mackintosh. He looked briefly into the merry, watery eyes. He smelt onions and beer.

'Mr Parker,' he said. 'This is a great—'

'Well, Edward? Remember me?' The deep, cultured voice was only slightly slurred; the face broke out in a volcanic smile, showing bad teeth. 'It's seventeen, eighteen years. I grant you that.'

Edward said, 'Ah.' He wanted to communicate, but had no words. It was like trying to be intelligent with a dentist. He nodded vigorously and, with his mouth open on the 'Ah', looked both stupid and alarmed.

'Doll Ferguson's,' Parker said. His eyes were bright with amusement and the beer dried out of them. 'What a party.'

'A party?' He searched, eagerly over the man's appearance – large ears, big nose, heavy shoulders, womanish, streaked hair. He felt sure Parker had not spent the night in bed. 'Doll Ferguson's? ... My God, *Parker*! Patrick Parker! Why the hell didn't I realise?' He performed many gestures rapidly. He struck his forehead with the palm of his hand, held out his arms on either side of Parker's shoulders, as though measuring them; snapped his fingers, waved; finally subsided into the swivel chair, his hands hanging limp over the arms, in a sprawled, boyish attitude. 'Parker!' he panted. 'Of course! Sit down, man. Why in God's name didn't I realise?'

'I don't see why you should,' Parker said modestly.

'But of course! Patrick Parker! My dear boy, I'm most dreadfully sorry.'

'That's all right,' Parker said.

'It must be this Thess. Thess.' He became business-like with the pages on his desk. The manuscript of *Lilac Moon*, some four hundred pages long, could in fact be found without difficulty. 'You never used to be called Thess.'

'True,' Parker said, unhelpfully.

'Well, now, what happened to Doll Ferguson? Tell me. Whatever happened to her?'

Parker was digging in his pocket. Edward jumped up with the cigarette box, manipulated the table lighter, pushed forward the weighty ash-tray.

'Gassed herself,' Parker said. He took three small darts, fitted with suction pads, out of his pocket and fixed them to the edge of Edward's desk. From time to time he hit them with the side of his finger so that they shuddered.

'How terrible,' Edward said. 'When?'

'Oh, about ten years ago. Poor old Doll. Did it in my flat, too.'

'How perfectly dreadful. Why?'

'She couldn't settle down after the *Gargoyle* changed hands. Said she felt homeless.'

'No – I mean why did she – I mean, why in your flat?'

'Oh that. They'd cut her off. Even the Water Board. Poor old Doll. We had good times there, Edward.'

'Yes,' Edward said. 'Yes, we did.'

Slowly, they smiled at each other. The moment of companionship brought tears to Edward's eyes. He forgot that the only thing he could truthfully remember about Parker was his name.

'It's good to see you,' he said gruffly. 'Why didn't you contact me all these years?'

'Complications,' Parker said. 'You know how it is. Didn't really feel justified until I'd finished this thing here. Then I thought, well, why not? He may be the guiding light of Batman's, he may be the literary lion-tamer, the Svengali of a dozen or more delicious little typing Trilbies – to me he's still wild young Teddy Knight, the life and soul of many an innocent orgy in years gone by. Teddy is the lad for you, Parker, I said. He won't have changed.'

Edward had hardly followed this. He took a short cut and arrived simultaneously with Parker at the last phrase, the one he understood.

'And have I?' he asked.

'Have you what?'

'Changed.' He set up, with an indrawn breath, all his defences. Where there had been open house there were now narrow slits through which he aimed at Parker, sitting on the outside.

Parker took his time. He looked at the ceiling, at the booklined walls, at the dubious Cézanne. Then, conscientiously, he sited Edward. The hair thinned on Edward's scalp; his stomach ballooned slowly; the flesh on his face grew heavier; his mind emptied itself of everything but longing.

'No ...' Parker said. 'No. A little more ...' His hands described an arc over his own concealing raincoat. 'Otherwise, I would say, much the same.'

Edward almost laughed. He felt full of energy. He offered the cigarettes again, and when it was all done stood in front of the electric fire patting the backs of his legs and looking quizzically through his own smoke at Parker.

'I'm forty-two,' he said. 'My daughter's seventeen. I don't know about you, but there are times when I find it depressing.'

'How about me?' Parker said, wrenching a dart off the desk and aiming it at Edward. 'I'm a grandfather. Hold still now.' The dart stuck, with a sickening thud, to Edward's temple. The impact made him stagger. He could feel it quivering there like a dreadful leech. 'Ha!' he barked. 'Good shot!' He tore it off and sent it whizzing back. Parker, experienced, ducked. For a few minutes they ran about the room, playing. Then Parker was seized with a terrible fit of coughing and for a moment, hovering over him, Edward thought he was going to die.

'Take it easy,' he said.

'Drink!' Parker gasped.

'Water?' Edward was at the bell.

'Good God, man . . . have you no whisky?'

'But of course, of course.' Breathless himself, his hands trembling with solicitude, he poured two large glasses of Scotch. In a few moments the gasping and blowing and shuddering had died down. Still rather breathless, they were back in their seats. The atmosphere was now definitely convivial. It's almost a party, Edward thought – incredulous but hopeful, like a woman who, in late middle age, gets her foot trodden on under the table.

'We should talk about the book,' he said quickly. 'It's a remarkable achievement.'

'Later,' Parker said. 'We'll grab a sandwich somewhere.'

'All right,' Edward said.

'What I always remember about you is that night you drank a bottle of sherry straight off and Doll pawned your grandfather's watch to pay for the cleaning.'

'Good Lord,' Edward said, 'I'd forgotten that.'

'What a party. Remember Philippa, that little blonde from the C.O.I. – she used to write a bit for *Horizon*.'

'I thought it was *Our Time*,' Edward said. 'Whatever happened to her?'

'I don't know,' Parker said. 'I thought you might know.'

'Have another?'

'Thanks. It's this bloody asthma. I'm really a beer-drinking man.'

'I can't stand beer,' Edward said.

'Ulcers?'

'Weak bladder.'

'Too bad. But wait – didn't she end up in the Crown Film Unit?'

'Who?'

'Philippa.'

'No,' Edward said, with absolute conviction. 'You're thinking of Janice Fairweather. I vividly remember that girl. She went off with Ian Macdougall to Wales.'

'Dylan was always kind to me,' Parker said. 'Whatever they say about him, he always treated me with the utmost courtesy. And after all, there was no need. Funny thing. I never felt the same about Auden.'

'No,' Edward said. 'I never felt the same about Auden either.'

'We ought to have a party,' Parker said. 'To celebrate.'

'Ah,' Edward sighed.

'We'll have it in your house. You live in Eaton Square?'

'St John's Wood.'

'Better. Ask a few friends round. Tell them to bring their own booze. Just what they can lay their hands on, nothing elaborate. What do you say?'

Edward nodded happily. The question seemed entirely rhetorical. His deep depression, the unexpectedness of Parker, the drink so early in the day had thrown him quite off balance. He vaguely recalled that there were things he had to do, people he had to see. But he didn't want to wake up. He was soothed, he was at peace, he was resting. 'Splendid,' he murmured. 'I'll ask Charmian.'

'Fine. I'll bring some people along.'

'Charmian's my daughter. I'll tell her to ask some friends. I don't know them very well. In fact, to tell you the truth, I don't know them at all. However, they seem to have parties of their own. Charmian' – he blurted it out suddenly, not meeting Parker's eye – 'Charmian has never had a party.'

'Never?'

'Well, not since she was fourteen.'

'Why on earth not?'

'I don't know,' Edward said. 'We don't seem to be geared to it.'

'You mean you don't . . .?'

'No,' Edward said. 'We lead a quiet life.'

Sympathy. It was the first time he had felt it in years. A short while ago he had felt himself growing old. Now his trousers shrank, his wrists jutted from his sleeves; he cast down his eyes and scrubbed at the Turkey carpet with the toe of his polished brown shoe.

'You poor sod,' said Parker softly. 'But you went to them all.'

'I know.'

'First to come and last to go. I remember it well. You could have lasted a marathon.'

'Well, there it is,' Edward said.

'We'll talk about it,' Parker said. 'Let's go round to the pub.'

'I can't,' Edward said, without conviction.

'You can and you will,' Parker said. 'This is important.'

'No man is an island,' Edward said, with a faint return of spirit.

'Exactly. We'll see what we can do.'

At ten o'clock that night, when they arrived home, Cecily turned off the oven, went straight to her bedroom and locked herself in. At half-past one Pip Rickards, an old mutual friend whom they had discovered in one of Parker's drinking clubs, walked out into the fog with a clothes-line he had found, neatly coiled by Cecily, in the broom cupboard. He spent ten minutes blundering about looking for a lamp-post on which to hang himself. An intelligent solicitor, one of Edward's friends, pursued him up and down, earnestly attempting to dissuade him from breaking the law. 'I refuse to be a witness,' he protested. 'I positively refuse to be involved.' Edward and Parker watched them with benign smiles from the open doorway. Finally Rickards hit the solicitor, who ran away, leaving his overcoat behind. He never claimed it, and the following day wrote a short note declining any further work from Batman's. Since he was an expert on the law of libel, both decent and obscene, this was a loss from which the firm never fully recovered.

Parker made a lasso out of the clothes-line and captured one of Charmian's friends as she was escaping out of the back door. Quite unaccountably, she burst into tears. Parker, a kind-hearted man, was dreadfully upset. He gave her a kiss to cheer her up. She said to Charmian, who was going quietly about with a dustpan and brush, 'Thank you for asking me. I hope I never have to speak to any of you again.' Charmian brought out the Hoover and began to clean up the hall.

Downstairs, in Edward's study, the older, sprightlier people were dancing. The gramophone records were

Charmian's. They were intended for devout listening and went on interminably.

'Come and dance,' Edward said to a girl with a long red pigtail, who was looking frightened.

'Are you mad?' she asked.

'But you haven't a drink—'

'I don't drink.'

'What *do* you do?'

'Nothing.'

'Well – what would you like to do?' He was reckless. He had taken his jacket off and undone the top three buttons of his shirt.

'Go home to bed,' she said.

She left him. He seized a large woman with fur boots on and jumped about with her for a bit, keeping his knees bent and his mouth open as though engaged in some curious form of goal-keeping.

'You're awfully good at this,' she panted. 'Where did you learn?'

'Just relax,' he said, bundling her under his arm.

Sometime later, he missed Charmian. He was suddenly anxious. Parker was hypnotising the Sales Manager's wife in the kitchen.

'Sleep . . .' he was murmuring. 'Sleep . . .' And flat out on the lino, the exhausted woman – she had four children and an Italian with laryngitis – slept.

'Where's Charmian?' Edward demanded.

'Sssh!' they hissed, turning on him. 'Thess is hypno-tising everyone.'

He found her in bed, holding the pillow round her ears.

'I hope you enjoyed yourself,' he said humbly.

She said, 'It will take a lot of explaining.'

'But it's a good party. Don't you like parties?'

'I hope it's not going to happen again.'

'What's wrong with you? You and your mother.'

'Please,' she said icily, turning her back on him. 'Do you mind? I don't know about you, of course, but I have to get up in the morning.'

It hurt him, but not deeply. He closed the door with a slight bang, to show his feelings. He spent the next hour imploring people not to leave. But they all had homes, it seemed, except Parker.

'I'll just doss down on the sofa,' Parker said. 'Your wife won't mind?'

'Not a bit,' Edward said. 'You can borrow my razor.'

'What a party. I'm sorry your wife was tired.'

'Yes,' Edward said. 'She gets tired.'

'Probably her age,' Parker said.

'You know,' Edward said, 'I sometimes feel I've wasted my life. I sometimes feel it's all been a bloody great mistake.'

'Don't despair,' Parker said. 'You've got the world at your feet, boy.'

'Thanks,' Edward said. 'Thanks, Parker.'

• • •

The publication of *Lilac Moon* was fixed for the second week in September. During those seven months, Edward was happier than he had been at any time in the last eighteen years. He seemed to himself entirely renewed. Looking back on his life, it occurred to him that he had lived over half of it in a state of fear.

Cecily said to him, 'Unless you face the fact that you are having a nervous breakdown, I shall leave you. I mean it, Edward.'

'Breakdown or break-up,' he said. 'What a depressing choice.'

'And have treatment,' she insisted. 'Proper treatment.'

Parker, on the strength of his advance, had taken a small flat in Camden Town. On the same day of his conversation with Cecily, Edward was cooking bacon and eggs for Parker in Parker's bathroom. He was being talked to, as he did this, by a girl named Emma. She sat on the edge of the bath, in which Parker kept his stores – half a packet of spaghetti, a tin of Instant Coffee and a few soft onions.

'My wife,' he said, 'doesn't understand me.'

'No?' Emma asked.

Edward threw back his head and laughed. He roared with laughter. 'By God,' he shouted, 'it's true! She doesn't!'

'You're crazy,' Emma said.

After that, with elaborate deceit, they shared Emma. It was very satisfactory, while it lasted. Edward recaptured his sense of alarm, so frustrated by Cecily. He made every conceivable difficulty for himself, arranging to meet her as far away as Fulham or Palmers Green. He wondered how he had possibly survived for so long without jealousy (he found it very hard to be jealous of Parker, but managed it somehow), and without guilt. Parker, who acted as father-confessor to Emma, even about himself, was happy to co-operate. It made Emma less demanding and gave him a kindly hold over Edward. Not that it was necessary to hold Edward. He clung. But Parker was not unaware that there were certain dangers in launching himself before the public for the first time at the age of fifty-five. It was pleasant to feel that everything possible would be done to help him.

In this spirit of fatherly concern, Parker devoted a great deal of his time to Batman's. He set himself up a small camp in Edward's office – an armchair, a bottle of Scotch, a few toys, a tin of cough sweets – and there he would read manuscripts, advise on dust-covers, give creative criticism to any visiting author who seemed to need it. Most of them did. In this way, Edward increased his list by four Cambridge undergraduates ('Don't worry about their politics,' Parker said. 'It's the voltage that counts.'), one professional house-breaker, two retired schoolmasters and a riding instructress. He also lost his only two best-sellers, his secretary, his Sales Manager (whose wife was now being hypnotised daily, at five guineas a time) and three promising young editors.

'Publishing is a racket,' Parker said. 'Why don't you get out of it? Try something creative for a change.'

'I hardly think,' Edward said, with surprising asperity, 'that this is quite the time.'

That evening, remembering it was laundry day, he went home. He found Cecily packing.

'What are you doing?' he asked.

'I'm leaving you.'

'But isn't that rather pointless – I mean, since I'm so seldom here?'

'So you admit it. You actually admit it.'

'Of course. Where did you put the laundry?'

'Charmian left three days ago.'

'Really? Why?'

'We don't feel safe any longer.'

'I'm sorry. Where did you say you put the laundry?'

'I asked you to have treatment. I told you you were ill.'

'I've never been better in my life.'

'What are you trying to do, Edward? What are you trying to do?'

'Just have a good time,' he said, smiling gently.

'And what about us? What about your wife and daughter?'

'You have a good time too,' he said.

The next day, after a long, enjoyable discussion, Parker gave up his flat and moved to St John's Wood. It was more convenient in every way. Emma had Charmian's room and gave simple little parties there for friends of her own age. Edward and Parker cooked the breakfast in turns, unless someone stayed for the night, in which case, of course, it was up to them. The char gave up coming because no one was ever awake to let her in, and she didn't like to have a key in case her handbag got stolen and then she would be held responsible. The laundry gave up coming because there was no one to answer the bell. Edward took his and Parker's shirts to the launderette. It took up a great deal of time. On Sundays they would do the week's washing up while listening to the Critics. Emma mended the fuses and did a bit of digging in the garden. She was a country girl, born and bred in the Cotswolds. She planted some mustard and cress, and one day they had it in sandwiches for lunch.

'She had green fingers,' Parker said, squeezing her.

'Oh,' she snapped, 'stop pawing me.'

It was the first sign of rebellion. After that, when they asked her where she had been, she always answered, 'To get some fresh air. London kills me.' Later, in the summer, she bought a polka-dotted headscarf and went off hop-picking. Finding, when she reached Kent, that the whole thing was mechanised, she settled in Canterbury. They had a postcard from her, telling them this, but since she gave no address they were unable to reply.

Meanwhile, in those teacups where such storms break, *The Lilac Moon* was rising. It was, in fact, a good book. Parker had talent, all the stronger for its total lack of use. Anyone who was anyone read the proof. It was unanimously acclaimed on the grounds that it was both tough and charming, nostalgic and prophetic, contemporary and in the direct tradition of the English novel. It was all things to all men, and to gather in the stragglers – girls, football players, university dons and the like – Parker let it be known that Batman's were having trouble with obscenity.

'You're overdoing it,' Edward said. 'The libraries are getting cold feet.'

'It's your job to reassure them,' Parker said, unwrapping a bright new water-pistol. 'Not mine.'

August was hot, and for the first time in eighteen years Edward did not take a holiday. Apart from the ceaseless work of talking about *The Lilac Moon*, he did very little. On his brisker days, he would appear in the office around twelve, make a few telephone calls, then hurry over to the pub for lunch. Before Parker, he had never frequented pubs. He had never felt this sense of coming home – the pampas grass in the hearth, the morning polish; the names Courage and Watney, Worthington and Bass, reminding him of some yeoman age, a kind of Elizabethan period of his life which he had never, in fact, known. Parker was always already at the bar, his furrowed, kindly face buried in a pint glass. 'Have a banger, boy,' he would say. At closing time, generally leading a small posse of new friends, they made an orderly move to Soho. There, in one of a number of cool drinking clubs, they would spend the afternoon. By six o'clock the period of gestation was over; a party was born.

'It's an odd thing,' Edward said one night, waking up in an Earls Court studio, 'but since Emma left I haven't seen a soul under thirty.'

'Why did you call her Emma?' someone asked. 'Or were you a romantic at the time?'

'I don't remember,' Edward said. Half an hour later he woke up again. 'We lived in Hamilton Terrace,' he explained. But everyone had gone. He wept for a few minutes into the cheerless sofa – it was some sort of chintz, and recently resprung. His tears were no more than an overflow. He felt them spilling out of him in great effort-less bursts. In the morning, feeling more balanced, he cooked the breakfast and shaved, after a fashion, with a small, female razor.

When he got home, Parker was waiting for him. 'It's a fine thing, I must say, it's a very fine thing. You never sent a proof to M.G.M.'

'You shouldn't have missed that party,' Edward said. 'Brother!'

'We don't know where to contact you. We don't know where the hell you are. I am forced to spend the evening in the Westbury, a place I detest—'

'You shouldn't do that,' Edward said.

'And another thing. What about *Vogue*?'

'What about it?'

'You think they can't read on *Vogue*? You think they don't care about literature? Well, let me tell you—'

'I'm wrong,' Edward said.

'You're wrong,' Parker said.

'All right,' Edward said. He was watching the little bubbles rise out of his Alka Seltzer. 'Why don't you get an agent?'

'I will,' Parker said.

Two minutes later, vividly wrapped in a new overcoat, he put his head round the door.

'Can you recommend one?'

'No,' Edward said.

'I didn't think you were spiteful,' Parker reproached him.

They looked at each other.

'Pargeter,' Edward said.

'Thanks, boy.'

For a week or two – it was the end of August, the beginning of September – Parker came home around midnight and left again at nine. He walked very straight these days, and carried a sword-stick. Perhaps the extent of his self-confidence was shown in the fact that he seldom took the sword out of the stick; he contented himself with knowing that it was there.

One afternoon, Edward called in at the office. The place seemed full of strangers. One of them, who did not bother to remove his hat, served Edward with divorce papers. The grounds were cruelty, and adultery with a woman or women unknown.

That evening he made a new discovery. It was easier, cheaper and more comfortable to have parties alone. Travelling about London took time. He was a busy man. Besides, the whole thing was so insecure. Supposing he couldn't find any people? He couldn't attract people, like Parker. However many drinks he bought them, they didn't seem to warm to him in the same way. He was very tired. It was all much simpler if you didn't have to get up in the morning.

After this, he was intensely occupied. There was no time to go to Batman's, no time to open letters or get a new chequebook or visit the launderette. His only visitors were solemn representatives of Gas, Electricity and Metropolitan Water Boards. He found a stock of candles in the store cupboard; cooking was unnecessary. His credit with the off-licence still held, and from them he could get potato crisps, peanuts and the occasional Mars Bar.

One evening, as he shuffled round trying to wake himself up, he came upon Parker packing.

'What are you doing?' he asked.

'Leaving, boy. I've taken a small place in Chelsea. Give me a ring sometime.'

'Certainly,' Edward said. 'But why don't you stay here?'

'I think I ought to warn you,' Parker said, 'they're getting restive at the office.'

'I don't see why you don't stay. Why don't you stay?'

'Here's my address,' Parker said, handing him a neat new visiting card. 'Keep in touch, boy.'

'But we were having such a good time,' Edward said.

Parker tucked a pound note into Edward's dressing-gown pocket.

'Take care of yourself,' he said.

Shaved, clean-collared, dreadfully tired, Edward sat in his swivel chair. One by one, he opened the drawers of his desk and looked inside. There was nothing he wanted. Getting up, he moved, with short, painful steps, about the room. He could not decide to take anything away. Reaching the mantelpiece, he peered at a photograph of a girl with some pigeons. He dusted it with his sleeve and put it back.

A woman came into the room. She said kindly, 'If you have time before you leave, Mr Knight, Mr Parker would like to see you.'

'No,' he said. 'No, I don't think so. Thank you.'

But Parker was already there. He sprang lightly across the room in Harris tweed. His hair was crew-cut. He had been smiling for some time, showing new teeth.

'Well, Edward, well! How good to see you.'

'Thank you,' Edward said. He sat down.

'So you've packed it in at last. I'm glad for you, boy. I'm really glad.'

'Thank you,' Edward said.

'I told you you should try something creative. Now how about settling down in the country and tackling that book?'

'Which book?' Edward asked.

'I dare say we could arrange a reasonable advance. That is, of course, when we receive the manuscript.'

'I never had the faintest desire to write a book,' Edward said very carefully.

'You worry me, Edward. You don't seem to come to grips.'

'I don't,' Edward said. His eyes closed. He forced them open.

'It took me over twenty years to write that novel. Faith, that's what you need. Faith in yourself. And discipline.'

'That's true,' Edward said. He closed his empty brief-case and, gritting his teeth for a moment, ordered his legs to support him.

'What are you going to do?' Parker asked.

'I don't know.'

'I'm off to New York at the end of the week. Why don't you stay in my flat for a while?'

'I might,' Edward said.

'Here's the key. Come any time.'

'You're very kind.'

'I can afford to be,' said Parker simply.

The telephone rang. Parker answered it. 'New York,' he said. He slid into the swivel chair, waving his free hand. 'See you, Edward. 'Bye now.'

Out in the street, Edward looked left and he looked right. There was nothing to choose between them. He yawned enormously. He was vaguely surprised that he didn't require a drink. What did he require? Rest – but apart from that, heaven knows. In order to be a man of decision, you must have something to decide. There seemed to be no particular reason why he should not stand there for ever. His legs were weak, but he was quite comfortable otherwise. If they became weaker he could, perhaps, sit down.

A taxi drew up at the kerb and a woman got out.

'Why, Mr Knight!' she said. 'I heard you'd been ill. How are you?'

Edward smiled at her.

'I'm just popping in for a word with Thess. Isn't it wonderful, the success he's had? You must feel very, very happy and proud.'

Edward nodded, yawning again behind closed lips.

'Now you can take my taxi. That's nice.'

He climbed in without a word.

'Chelsea,' he said.

Parker's key opened the door of Parker's flat. Edward wandered round for a little while turning the lights on and off, like a child at the Science Museum. He cleaned his teeth, using Parker's dentifrice. He took a drink of water from the tap. He rang up the Time.

'I'm tired,' he said. 'I'm tired. I'm tired.'

Then he spoke to himself. 'Silly boy,' he said. 'You've been burning the candle at both ends.'

Moving slowly, with care, like a man locking up for the night, he turned on all the gas fires and the oven and the burners, curled up on the sofa and settled down for an eternity of sleep.

THE WHITE RABBIT

Now there's no longer anyone to talk to, I want to try telling this story of the rabbit in my own way. I want to tell it for my own purpose. I believe that if I can find someone who will understand it, they will also understand me. They will realise that I'm not the same as other girls of my age. I am not someone to be taken lightly. I am not a silly rubber ball to be kicked around for a few days, thrown up in the air, lost and left for someone else to discover. This is how most girls are, and they expect it. But I, Juliet Malleson, am not like that. I need to be understood.

Why are they all so stupid? God, how stupid they are. It's like beating against a brick wall, living. It's like prison. My stepfather has become fat and trivial. His eyes are like feather dusters. He has the look on his face of someone waiting, patient and resigned and timid, for an air raid to be over. My mother snivels into her handkerchief and then turns on me with a face like wet blotting-paper and offers to lend me her new handbag or her mink stole. What on earth do I want her mink stole for? Where does she think I go in the evenings? What does she think I do?

I suppose they're haunted. The fact that they have made me what I am is a thing that they never for one moment forget. I knew this from the very beginning but now – now I'm brought up and there's nothing more they can do – I can see it killing them. I don't mean actually, but inside. I am an incurable disease, which they bear with fortitude.

They don't talk about me anymore. They don't tell people about me. My mother's letters are so boring nowadays that I don't bother to read them, and when I go out on the balcony at night all I hear through their bedroom window are sighs and yawns and the hopeless sound of my stepfather gargling.

Just now, of course, they have another cross to bear. Dr Palethorpe has given me up. They had tremendous faith in him. I suppose they thought he was inexhaustible.

I think I did too. I always knew he wasn't doing any good, but I confess I got used to him. I spent so much time with him. I must have made hundreds of little cane baskets and clay pots for putting things in and painted heaven knows how many significant pictures for Dr Palethorpe to examine. There was no aggression in my painting, apparently. No conflict in my clay. I couldn't help it. I like everything to be neat. I always have.

I must have spent months of my life talking to Dr Palethorpe, but in the end I don't think he was much the wiser. I told him what I had for lunch yesterday and what somebody said to somebody else in the Middle School cloakroom and the plots of all the films I saw. Probably he just got bored. Anyway, he said the time had come to part. I don't mind. It was all damned stupid anyway. He suggested that I went to someone else, but I'm not going. It seems absurd for my stepfather to be paying out nine guineas a week just for me to be told that I'm the child of a broken marriage and suffering from insecurity. When they've finally proved this fact, they've finished with you. It's a waste of time.

I'm called Juliet Malleson, but my name is really Juliet Briggs. My father's name is Philip Briggs. The only time in my life I remember seeing him was on the day when he gave me this white rabbit. It was six years ago. Richard Malleson is my stepfather. He is the one who gargles and who waits, with such sadness, for some proof that he isn't guilty, some sort of last-minute reprieve. He won't get it. My father is the only one who comes off scot-free.

My stepfather and my mother and I live where we have lived for fourteen years, in a block of flats overlooking Hyde Park. The flats are expensive and have hydrangeas in brass cauldrons standing in the entrance hall. I don't remember living anywhere else. I don't remember my father living anywhere, except in this pit where I went to see him that day. He left it shortly afterwards. I suppose the rabbits all died. I think he has sold vacuum cleaners and Encyclopaedia Britannicas and some sort of preparation for taking wood-worm out of furniture. Also he has sold second-hand cars. Anything with a commission. My stepfather put up the money for this rabbit farm. I didn't know this at the time. It shows how my stepfather felt about paying – I mean for the fact that he and my mother and I were so fortunate, so happy.

My stepfather was always more gentle, more generous, more patient, more understanding, more loving than anyone else in the world. He paid twice over for everything. And yet now it seems as though he has got nothing in return.

He fell in love with my mother at the end of the war. They were made for each other, I can see that. They explained to me about the divorce. Apparently it was perfectly friendly except that my father, for some reason, insisted on being the Petitioner. For once, I suppose, he felt he had the right to a reputation. So my stepfather, who has never had so much as a parking summons in his life, became a co-respondent. I shouldn't think they had even committed adultery at the time. They were both very anxious not to harm me and if my mother kissed my stepfather she immediately kissed me too, so that I shouldn't feel overlooked or neglected in any way.

I loved them so much.

Did I tell him this? Perhaps I'd forgotten it.

But you can't forget the experience of loving. You can only push it back and cover it up and use it for something else. I loved them so much. It was like carrying a secret honour or being filled with the holy spirit. These are not things I believe in, or would ever say to anyone like Palethorpe. The truth is that all my childhood was an experience of loving, a continuous miracle. If this has happened to you, you are different from other people. It's no good pretending you aren't. You are quite different.

I suppose it seems ridiculous that anyone of seventeen can talk like this about their childhood. After all, it wasn't so long ago. But once you have stopped being a child, you might as well be a hundred, it doesn't make any difference. Childhood is the first thing you realise you will never have again.

My stepfather was an extremely clean man. He still is, I suppose, but I don't notice it as I used to. The cuffs of his shirts were blue-white and held together by flat gold links. He had very thin ankles and rather big feet. His socks never wrinkled and were always plain navy or black, never wool. He was unable, I think, to wear wool next to his skin.

His hands were big too, the nails like pale, polished counters. He wore soft leather gloves and a short grey overcoat which was proofed in some way against the rain.

You could never imagine my stepfather in a mackintosh or putting up his umbrella. He was not the sort of man to get caught in the rain, or by any foreseeable accident. It was not that he was cautious but that everything naturally went right for him. He believed that there was an answer to everything, provided you had the patience and devotion to find it. He was not soft. He had thousands of people working for him, and a Picasso and a Renoir hanging in his office. But he was dedicated to understanding. Those are the words that come. It is not so much the words, but the feeling of the words I mean.

My mother never quite matched him. There was a nervousness about her which, even with him, didn't entirely disappear. I don't remember her before she married him, but I suppose it was this inadequacy, this fuss she was always about to make, that was the reason for her marrying my father. When I asked her why she married my father, she got flustered. I could see then that she was the sort of person who makes mistakes, leaves things in the middle; the sort of person who can never fill a hot-water bottle without scalding themselves. I despise people like this. I can't bear inefficiency. I can't stand untidiness. Perhaps I should have despised my mother if she had stayed married to my father, and then everything would have been different anyway. I should probably be dead by now.

I never thought about my father. I knew he existed but he was quite unreal, like some remote relation you will never see. When I was eight I wrote on the wall by my bed, *Juliet Malleson, 85 Malleson House, Malleson W.C.2, Great Malleson, the Continent of Malleson, the Hemisphere of Malleson, Malleson World, Malleson Universe, Malleson Space. Signed by order of Juliet Malleson.* I think I felt that things like this were expected of me. They were pleased. They admired it. They never told me that anything I did was wrong. It stayed on the wall until I was eleven, when they had the room done up in pink roses and muslin drapes and gave me a dressing-table set with JM engraved on the backs of the brushes and the hand mirror.

I was eleven when I got this idea that if I tried hard enough, really devoted myself to it every minute of the day and night, I could be my stepfather – and also, indirectly, my mother. It sounds silly now, but it was no sillier than believing you could be invisible, or fly or walk through walls. I'd tried all these things and I believed that the only reason I had failed was that it wasn't absolutely necessary to do them. You could get on without doing them. I couldn't get on without my stepfather. If I was never going to have to leave him – and my mother, of course – if nothing was ever going to come between us, then I would have to become them. It seemed to me obvious. There was no other way. Unless I could identify myself with them – Palethorpe's word – they might, one day, leave me.

Well, how can you break in on people, force yourself into their heads? How can you feel, as they touch wood, the feeling of wood; taste, as they eat, the taste of what they are eating; see, as they turn and look at you, what they are seeing? It's impossible. I suppose it's what people pretend to do when they're in love, but it's impossible. They are wasting their time.

As they talked, I would talk with my lips and nod and frown and smile. When they kissed, I would press two fingers against my mouth. I spied on them. I hid under their bed, I read their letters, I listened outside their bedroom window at night. I touched their sheets and their clothes. I walked in step with them and at meals copied the way they ate, chewing, swallowing, drinking in the same moment. I pretended to be ill so that I didn't have to go to school, and when all the illnesses ran out I invented dozens of fears – fear of buses, fear of teachers, fear of the man who marked the tennis courts, fear of the brother of one of the girls who used to meet her from school with a catapult sticking out of his coat pocket. I knew that they would never tell me that anything I did was wrong. I knew that in case I should be jealous, and lose my feeling of security, they had never had a child of their own. When you know something like this you feel absolutely privileged. You can never go too far, because understanding is endless.

One night they came in, as they always did, to say good night to me. It was summer, and although my mother drew the curtains the room was still full of deep pink sunlight.

My stepfather sat down on the edge of my bed and held his hand against my face. His hand smelt very faintly of Verbena. My mother leant over the end of the bed. I could tell that she was more than usually flustered.

My stepfather asked how it was going. He meant my transmigration. Naturally, I had told them what I was trying to do. They seemed to think it was possible.

I said it was going all right and told him that I had read somewhere that deep breathing was very important.

My mother said, 'But won't it be very boring for us? I mean, we'll only have each other to talk to. Won't we miss you?'

I said of course not. On the contrary, I should be there all the time. Why have three people, I asked, when you need only have two?

My stepfather said, 'But, Julie, don't you want to have a life of your own?'

I said no, I didn't see any point in having a life of my own.

We got up. My face felt bare, as though it had lost a warm covering. He said, 'The trouble is, it's going to be so awkward for other people. Supposing they want to see you?'

I didn't care about other people. Who, for instance?

My mother opened her mouth and shut it again. She looked at my stepfather as though she had just broken something, or asked people to dinner on the wrong night.

He said, 'Well. Your father, for instance.'

I said, oh, him. He'd never want to see me anyway. I patted the bed and asked my stepfather to come and sit down again. He didn't come. The pink light flushed their faces so that they seemed in some curious way to be ashamed.

'As it happens,' my mother said very quickly, 'he does want to see you. Naturally he wants to see you. He's coming to take you out.'

'On Sunday,' my stepfather said.

They waited, looking at me as though I was a tower on which they had placed the last, delicate brick. Of course I didn't know that they had asked my father to come; that they had worried themselves into thinking that this transmigration of mine was some terrible symptom of the artificial life they had forced upon me. I didn't know that they had decided that I needed my father. They were falling back on him like enlightened parents fall back on comforters and night-lights and Red Riding Hood. They thought their love had failed me and that now, however reluctantly, they must accept nature. It was hard for them. As hard, I suppose, as cutting off your arm and saying it belongs to somebody else.

But I didn't know any of this, and since they had always been so open and, it seemed to me, natural about the situation between us and my father, I didn't understand why they seemed to be so nervous.

I said well, that was all right. I should still be here on Sunday. But why did he have to take me out? Why couldn't he see me in the flat?

'He runs a rabbit farm,' my stepfather said, as though this explained it.

'You'd like to see the rabbits,' my mother said. 'Angoras. They're very sweet.'

I said I didn't like rabbits much, but provided I didn't have to stay long, I didn't mind.

I didn't suspect anything. I trusted them. They seemed very pleased, but also bewildered. I had the impression that they had expected this conversation to go on for a very long time. Now it was over so soon we were left with nothing to say, like people saying goodbye on a railway station.

'Well . . .' my mother said. Her eyes darted about the room and she kept biting her lip as though something was jabbing into her.

My stepfather said, 'We must have Venetian blinds in this room. The child can't possibly go to sleep in broad daylight.'

I can hear him now, controlling my mother and the sun and my love for him. Thinking he had controlled my love for him.

But why should he want to control it? It was natural. He had spent seven long years, like Jacob, encouraging it to grow. Why did we have to stunt it and twist it to suit some theory that ought to be true, ought to be right?

Everything that happened after that was mock, sham, artificial. Everything we did was unreal. We were like dogs with parasols or monkeys having nursery tea. But why? That is what no one ever explained. Why did it have to happen?

My father arrived on Sunday morning. He didn't come up to the flat. My mother was watching out of the window and said in a fussed voice, 'He's here, darling. Are you ready?'

I was wearing a green and white striped dress and my new nylon petticoat and white socks and sandals. I took a white cardigan, in case it got cold later on. My hair was long then and I wore it in two fat, glossy pigtails tied at the end with green ribbon. I remember feeling clean all over, between my toes, under my fingernails, behind my ears: clean everywhere, and smelling of Verbena. My mother always bought Verbena bath soap. It hung on the end of a silk cord, a huge, smooth lemon.

I said Yes, I was ready. We went down in the lift. It was so early that there was a heat mist on the park and nobody about but a few people walking their dogs and one man all alone swimming his horse through the waves of white fog.

My father was sitting in this very small car like a grown-up crouched inside a toy. He was very thin and wore a shortsleeved shirt that flapped round his elbows. And braces. Now, when I try to remember him, all I can think of is the fact that his shoulders were perpetually hunched as though trying to relieve the strain of these braces.

At the time I may have looked at him and thought, 'This is my father. My mother was once married to this man.' I don't know. All I remember is my mother saying, 'Have a lovely time, darling. And don't, *please*, bring back a rabbit!'

She laughed as she said it. I knew it was a false and wretched laugh. I felt sorry for her, but it was too late by then. She should have let me feel sorry for her earlier. I could have realised, if I had ever been told, that her life had not been easy. She never showed me until then, when she stood on the steps waving goodbye and we were rattling off down the Bayswater Road. My father and I. But I didn't think of us like that. I held down my dress, because it was an open car, and I remember shouting, 'What a funny car this is,' and he shouted, 'What's funny about it?' and I shouted, 'Nothing, I suppose. But Daddy has a Jaguar.'

My father, then as now, was insignificant. I only remember seeing him once in my life, on this day which made a chasm between my childhood and my age. However melodramatic this may sound, it is true. The day, the place, can never be forgotten. Only my father remains vague and unrecognisable. We spent the day separately, except for a meal which we ate around three in the afternoon. For the rest of the time he left me to explore my background – I suppose that is what I was meant to be doing.

This is how I describe it now. I climbed round the pit in which he festered; I smelled it; I accumulated it behind my knees, in the grooves of my elbows; it gathered in all the private, Verbena-scented parts of my body. In a few hours I discovered everything that my parents had kept securely down drains, locked in enamel and zinc and the sweet disguise of Air-Wick. I discovered what they had been protecting me from.

It was no more, to tell the truth, than a scatter of old eggshells, a blaze of flies over a couple of gaping dustbins; a noon buzzing with disease; a cinder path which burned the crêpe soles of my sandals; four dead rabbits in a dark hut where a hundred more rocked their long, mean heads behind the wire netting. It was not a grown-up's idea of hell, which is a place of ideas and endless, calculated disappointments. But to me it was unbearable.

What I think of as a pit was really a small valley, opening out into a flat space enclosed by high, wooded banks. A long wooden hut ran along one side of it. On the other side was another, smaller hut with a veranda. Both huts were built on concrete legs. A rough cinder path had been made between them. The sun fitted exactly over the rim of this pit. Once in the pit there was no escaping the sun. It stared straight down on you. There was not a shadow, not a place where it was cool or dark or did not smell of dying. My father sat in a basket chair on the veranda. Apparently he could afford to drink whisky all day. I had never hated anyone before. I kept thinking that it would soon be over.

What I felt may have been no more than disgust at the dirt, which I had never known before, and natural horror at the four rabbits which had been dead for some time and were now, in the most terrible way, living. Any child would have felt the same. It was nothing to do with me, any more than my father was anything to do with me. But I hated him. I was so angry. The thought that he believed he was my father made me sick; I mean physically sick.

I said, 'Four of those rabbits are dead. You don't look after them, do you?'

He said, 'What d'you mean dead? I look after those rabbits. Himalayans, worth a bloody fortune. When a rabbit's asleep it looks dead. Can't tell the difference.'

I said that these were full of maggots.

He looked at me and told me to go and clean myself up. I think he was frightened. I couldn't wash, because I couldn't find any water. I did what I could, and when I came back he wasn't on the veranda. He was wandering across the floor of the pit with his shoulders hunched up, coming towards me with his hands – they were thick and red, all his fingers the same thickness, with stray black hairs on the knuckles – cupped round something that needed enormous care. He looked down at his hands as he tried to keep to the cinder path. I stood at the top of the wooden staircase with my cardigan ready and my hair ribbons freshly tied. As he reached the bottom of the staircase he held out his hands to me. He was holding this white rabbit. It quivered so much that I thought it would shake itself out of his hands.

He said, 'It's for you.'

I said, 'But I don't want it.'

He said, 'Look, it's only a baby. I never gave you a present. It's a fine rabbit. Worth a lot of money.'

I said, 'They told me not to take one home.' I was crying. I hardly ever cried when I was a child.

He said, 'Come on, Julie. I never gave you a present before. What are you crying for? Go on. Take it.'

I don't know what else I could have done. I took it. It was a horrible creature, small and thin and bald under its long, dirty hair. It breathed without any noise and it scrabbled in my lap with its long, sharp feet as though it wanted to jump away. It was awful to have to touch it.

All the way back to London my father sang, in a tuneless sort of voice. I knew he was glad the day was over. I kept rehearsing what my stepfather would say. I knew he wouldn't think of letting me keep the rabbit, but I was not sure of the voice or the words he would use. This worried me. I felt I should know. The rabbit crouched in my lap. It was so frightened I hoped it would have a heart attack and die. On the other hand I was longing for my father to see how firmly, how strongly my stepfather would repudiate it. Forcing that horrible, creeping, nibbling rabbit of yours, he would say, on my Julie. How dare you? It wasn't the sort of thing my stepfather would say, but the feeling behind it was all right.

I almost began to feel sorry for my father. I said, as we passed Olympia, 'They won't let me keep it, you know.'

He said, 'We'll see about that. I'm not going to have any daughter of mine deprived of the company of animals. It's not natural.'

I let it pass, about being his daughter. After all, it didn't matter. I said, 'Well, I'm telling you. They won't let me keep it.'

He said threateningly, 'We'll see about that.'

It was almost dark by the time we got back. The park was like a hushed forest and the clean streets glistened like rivers. I was never so glad, never so grateful for my home.

I told him he'd better come up. So he followed, shambling along and pretending he didn't see the hydrangeas and not remarking on the cool air, the soft carpets, the hum of the lift as it took us up in that clean, safe building. I was carrying the rabbit, which kept trying to run about in the crook of my arm. When we got to the front door I rang four times. My father hung about by the lift shaft. My mother opened the door and was followed immediately by my stepfather. They both held out their hands to me. They were so glad to welcome me back. I couldn't go to them, because I was holding the rabbit. I held out my nursing arms. It didn't seem necessary to explain.

They both peered down. Their faces went quiet, and they didn't say anything.

My father mumbled behind me, 'I gave it to her. It's a present. How are you, Malleson?'

My stepfather said, 'Fine. I'm fine.'

They looked from me to my father and then at each other and then back to the rabbit. I said, 'I told him you wouldn't let me keep it.'

My mother said, 'Not let you?' and laughed, glancing at my stepfather. My stepfather said, 'It's very kind of you, Briggs. We'll fix up a hutch somewhere.'

I couldn't believe it. I heard my mother saying, 'Julie will love having a pet. It's perfectly natural she should want one. Thank you, Philip. It was very thoughtful.'

'But you don't understand,' I said carefully. 'I don't want it. I do not want to have a rabbit.' I held it out in my hands, to show them exactly what a hateful thing it was.

There was a very short silence. It took them a moment or two to decide what was best for me. As they did so, their faces softened. My mother scooped the rabbit out of my hands and held it against her black dress. My stepfather put his arm round me and pushed me gently inside the flat. As he closed the door I heard him saying to my father, 'I'll show you downstairs, Briggs. We're very grateful to you for . . .'

When he came back he fixed up a temporary hutch out of an orange box and a net curtain. Behind this net curtain the rabbit did not move. My mother gave it lettuce and raw carrot. I refused to go near it. I refused to talk about it. When they came to say good night they kept telling me how tomorrow they would buy a proper hutch and we would clean the rabbit and give it a name. They suggested Galahad. I never asked them why.

When my stepfather kissed me I didn't kiss him back or touch him. What was the good? It was clear that he believed I was my father's child. He allowed me to keep a rabbit given to me by my father. I no longer belonged to him.

And if I didn't belong to him, I was alone.

I had never been alone before. It was extremely frightening. I lay there so frightened at the idea that I could never really belong to my stepfather that my heart drummed all over my body. When I got out of bed my knees were shaking and I was sweating. I thought perhaps I had caught some disease from the pit, from the dead rabbits. I would die too, but this didn't comfort me. I didn't want revenge, or to make them sorry. I only wanted to be with them again; to continue, more urgently than ever, the efforts that had been interrupted by this terrible day.

I went out on to the balcony. They had gone to bed. They weren't talking. I watched the cars pouring up the Bayswater Road. The road looked like a string of lights winking and flashing between Marble Arch and Notting Hill. Our flat was on the tenth floor and sometimes, if you looked down long enough, the whole building seemed to be swaying. When I was small they had the balcony caged in with wire netting.

It's hard to describe love, but loneliness is even harder. I feel it now, perhaps almost as much as I did that night. But now there is nothing I can do about it. Now I know that you can't take things out of life, any more than you can put things into it. Everything that is there naturally, must belong. Nobody told me this. I know it because this is what we tried to do, and look at the result. We tried to put things in and take things out as though consequences, as though even common sense, didn't matter.

After a bit, I went and sat on my bed in the dark. It is easy to say now what I was thinking, and try to make it sound reasonable. It wasn't reasonable. I just thought over and over again: There are four people in this flat. Me. My stepfather. My mother. The rabbit. Four lots of breath. Four individuals to think about. Four instead of two.

I suppose it made sense in a way. The rabbit was part of my father and my parents had accepted this part of my father in their lives. In my life. Feelings like this come when you are a child, or when you have been alone for a long time. Perhaps they also come when you are mad. They begin as a stray thought, just a whisper, that happens to drift across your mind. Then, if you keep hold of it, repeat it over and over, concentrate on it, the thought begins to grow until you are filled with it, until the whole world is filled with it. After this what you do seems perfectly reasonable, but on a different level from ordinary reason and therefore, when the feeling is over, impossible to explain.

I don't know how long it was before I went into the kitchen and untied the net curtain. The rabbit was heaped up in the corner of the box. It was still trembling. When I took it out it kicked its back legs. Although it was small and unhealthy, it was very strong. I put one hand underneath it and one hand over it and held it away from me so that its fur wouldn't touch my night-dress. Then I went back through my bedroom on to the balcony. I reached out as far as I could over the railings and shut my eyes and let go of the rabbit. It was easy. There wasn't a sound, except for the traffic, which never stops. It was rather cold by then, and when I went back into my bedroom I put on my dressing-gown and slippers.

I went back into the kitchen and emptied the orange box of the dirt and lettuce and carrot and put it back in the store cupboard. I folded the net curtain and hid it under a cushion, because I didn't know where my mother had got it from. I opened the window a little. You couldn't tell there had ever been a rabbit. Then I went to the bathroom and washed my hands and cleaned my teeth. Then I went to sleep. I was happier than I had ever been in my life.

The next morning I got up and dressed for school. Sheila, the daily maid, got the breakfast. She didn't come on Sundays, so of course she didn't know about the rabbit. My parents always had breakfast in their bedroom. I had mine in the kitchen because I liked to talk to Sheila, who once won a gold medal for being the best woman roller-skater in Brixton.

After breakfast I went in to say goodbye to my parents. My mother was in bed. My stepfather, smelling cool and bitter, his hair beautifully brushed, was sitting at the table by the big window that showed nothing but sky. He was reading the *Manchester Guardian*, the only honest paper in the country.

He said, 'Well, Julie, how is your rabbit this morning?'

I said, 'I haven't seen it.'

I kissed them goodbye and went to school. There was nothing on the path or the gravel. I really believed that we could, after all, go on living as though my father and the rabbit had never existed.

I suppose that I thought that if I could tell this story to someone who understood it, I might get back into a world in which I was always loved, always approved of. Perhaps I still believe that there is someone who won't judge me as other people are judged. Someone, somewhere, who can say, 'I love Juliet Malleson whatever she has done, and it will be a privilege and a delight to care for her and protect her and rule her for ever.'

Anyway, this is what Dr Palethorpe might say. If it is true, it is not because I'm romantic but because I know exactly what I need. I do not need these failed and ruined people. Bits of their happiness still hang about the flat like something not properly cleared away. When I go into a room where they aren't expecting me there's always a moment, just as I come through the door and before they have looked round to see who it is, when I feel . . .

I feel I'm intruding. That's all. Bursting in on them as they pore over the remains. How quickly they hide them away. My stepfather's voice is flat and empty. 'Hallo, Julie. What have you been up to?' I don't answer him. He doesn't expect me to.

And yet, for heaven's sake, who cares about rabbits? A rabbit is nothing. They poison millions of them with myxomatosis. They beat them out of the fields with sticks. Anything that happened to one in connection with a rabbit is bound to be trivial. It can't be all that important. Nobody with any sense would think it mattered.

Then supposing, after I'd told this story, that all the person did was to laugh? Or yawn or say, 'Yes? What happened then?' Supposing they didn't believe me? Imagine looking into a blank face, with the story told and nothing more to say. Imagine knowing it hadn't worked – that all they had heard was a piece of somebody's life which meant, to them, absolutely nothing? I don't think I could bear it.

Perhaps it doesn't matter. Perhaps there are millions of people like me, doing the same things, feeling the same things, walking about without signs to make to each other, without signals.

Wouldn't it be ridiculous if you thought your navel was a deformity? If you didn't dare to undress? And there would be the whole world hurrying up and down streets and sitting down to tea with their stomachs secret and hidden, never thinking to mention the fact that they too . . .

But that isn't my idea. It's what Palethorpe said the other day, when he was saying goodbye to me. He shook my hand honestly and firmly, I suppose to show that we were parting friends.

'Wouldn't you think that was silly, Julie?'

And probably I said yes.

But it's not silly, for me. I am different from other people. I can't see how they expect me to behave like every-one else.

I am Juliet Malleson.

There must be someone who can understand me – someone whose patience will never end, whose care will be eternal, whose love will tolerate anything I do?

SECOND HONEYMOON

What are we *doing*? Frances asked herself, staring up at the ornate ceiling. What on earth do we think we're *doing*? Tears of exasperation, disappointment, shot to her eyes. Waking was the worst part of her day. What, she would demand of whatever stucco cherub, fly-blown lampshade, Technicolor Pieta that first met her eyes, what do we think we're *doing*?

Her husband, sensing trouble, came warily out of sleep, feeling his way from worry to worry – breakfast late, letters not come, bad dream (children dead or neglected), passports and travellers' cheques stolen; ill, perhaps; mosquitoes? At last, since she had not spoken, he arrived shakily at the point where he could open his eyes and take a quick look at the day.

As usual, the sky was blue; as usual, church bells rang like gongs; as usual, Vespas and Lambrettas ripped the early morning like calico. For a moment even he was not sure where they were – Pisa, Parma, Sienna, Florence, Turin, Milan?

'Well,' he said, pinning it down neatly, 'how does it feel to wake up in Rome?'

'Exactly as it feels waking up anywhere else.' Her head was turned away. He knew the expression of her face, burnt by tears, but refused to recognise it. He stretched, casually flinging an arm in her direction.

'Rome . . .' He longed to say the words 'Eternal City', but some rare sensibility, possibly left over from his dreams, prevented him.

'Well, what's so wonderful about it?' she asked, muffled. Then, before he could hurriedly cover himself, slop somehow into his armour of stupidity, she sat up in bed, flinging her arms high. 'What's so bloody wonderful about it?'

'Oh, Frances . . .'

'What do we think we're doing? What are we up to?' Her voice rose up and up as though somewhere, far beyond sound, it might break into a place of absolute peace, inaudibility. There was a knock at the door.

'*Entrate*,' Bernard called commandingly.

A waiter eased inside, flashed *Buon giorno*, slid dexterously across the uneven, polished floor to their bed.

'Breakfast?'

'*Grazie*,' Bernard said. '*Mille grazie*.'

'*Per favore, signore*.' Smiling straight at them, as though to convey some urgent but unspeakable good news, he went away.

'Why be so effusive?'

Bernard sighed and poured out the coffee. The sun struck directly on the threadbare scalp which he still maintained was a good head of hair.

'You don't say "a thousand thanks" to a waiter in English, do you?'

'I wasn't talking English.' He was hopeless, tired out already. 'Oh, I don't know.'

'What don't you know? What do you *mean* when you say you don't know?'

'I don't mean anything. Good heavens, Frances, I don't mean anything at all.'

'No,' she said, lying back on her pillows. 'That's true, at least. What on earth are we doing, that's what I want to know? We must be mad. Stark, staring mad . . .'

The first dreadful energy of waking, coming head-on with the day, had deserted her. She half lay, looking down into her coffee, the saucer supported on the gentle curve of her stomach. In this position the taut flesh under her chin folded, the skin drooped; the imperceptible flowering of age was at last visible under her cheeks and eyes. Bernard looked away.

'I suppose you don't want to go to St Peter's,' he said.

She groaned faintly.

'Or the Sistine Chapel.'

'I've *been* to the Sistine Chapel,' she said, in a tone of disgust.

'Of course.' Slowly, as he looked at the polished floor between his bare feet, his face became congested, visibly darkened. 'Of course one visit to the Sistine Chapel is enough. Lasts you a lifetime. One single visit. What did you see?'

'Nothing. I don't remember. My neck ached.'

'Why?'

'Oh, for heaven's sake, I don't know why! I just remember my neck ached! Really.'

'Obviously it made very little impression on you. The chapel, I mean.'

'No. It didn't. If you're so mad to see it, why not go?'

'Who were you with? Who took you?'

'What d'you mean – who took me? I wasn't a child, was I? Nobody *took* me.' She closed her eyes elaborately praying for patience. He noticed in the deep creases between her nose and mouth the sediment of some cream, hormonised face-pack, flakes of a youth-giving embrocation like crumbled whitewash.

'Oh God!' he shouted, making her open her eyes.

'What's the matter?'

'Nothing.'

He stamped rigidly towards the bathroom. As usual it was windowless, unventilated. The smell of hot water had become sickening to him. He left the door open while he shaved, making careless sweeps at his face with a blunt razor.

'I suppose it was that Swede?'

'Swede?' Her voice drifted lazily from the bedroom. He couldn't see her, but imagined her roused from some reverie, lying there with her chin on her chest; resting in his absence.

'Prix de Rome, wasn't he? That brilliant painter no one's ever heard of. That romantic genius with the bow-legs.'

There was a long silence. He drubbed his face, hoping to improve his circulation. At last she answered quietly. 'He didn't have bow-legs.'

'From the photograph,' he snarled, coming back into the room, 'he was bandy, hooped, practically a dwarf. Pity you didn't have better taste. Really, a pity.'

He began rummaging in the suitcase for a shirt. Her voice sounded strained, as though she were trying to swallow the sound it made. 'Look, it was a sketching party, a crowd of schoolgirls—'

'And the Swede?'

'He made a bit of money taking us to galleries, you know, museums. There was no harm in it.'

He stiffened, bent over the suitcase. 'You said that you weren't taken, that nobody took you!'

She did not answer. He felt that she was watching him. There were moments when she so powerfully humiliated him that it was all he could manage to drag himself out of her sight, into safety. Now, with his back turned, his foolishness exposed, her scorn threatened him. He knew, with ghastly despair, his pallid, pear-shaped back, the reedy legs, the sedentary stomach. He turned with furious pugnacity, driven to defend himself.

She was not looking at him. Her eyes were closed. Silently, with hardly a tremor of her face, she was crying. The tears welled out like great drops of glycerine and spilled singly over her face, lodging in the corners of her mouth, damping the soft, thin hair over her ears. It was a manifestation of great sorrow. He understood it, in so far as it concerned himself, but there was nothing he could do. Cold, sobered, dreary, he dressed.

'I'll wait for you downstairs,' he mumbled, leaving her, bolting before the dreadful clam of her misery could erupt, as he knew it might, and attack him.

Half an hour later she appeared in the lobby, trim and valiant. He admired her appearance and said, with some relief, 'You look very nice, darling.' She seemed not to hear, glancing vaguely and lightly round the lobby, settling the strap of her handbag over her thin wrist. He remembered then that she strongly disliked to be told that she looked nice. She was a woman who found it painful to break the habit of being exceptionally beautiful, perpetually young. The hyperboles of their early years eluded him. 'Beautiful,' he added rustily, and too late.

She smiled brilliantly at the desk clerk. 'Well?' she demanded, still smiling, 'Where are we going?'

The guide-book bulged Bernard's pocket; his camera hung, a contemptible insignia, round his neck.

'Well . . .' he said weakly, 'where would you like to go?'

'I don't mind. Where would *you* like to go?'

'Well . . .' Faced with the whole of Rome – the realisation of perhaps his last ambition – he was bewildered. Alone, he would have taken it slowly, inch by inch. He felt the obligation to be decisive, purposeful, and his spirit collapsed. He simply could not do it. 'After all,' he said, his voice rising a little, 'you know the place. You've been here before. You might at least make a suggestion.'

He didn't have to look at her. He knew how her face hardened.

'I don't mind,' she repeated, urgently and softly. 'I simply do not mind where we go!' She sped through the swing door and waited for him on the pavement. He saw himself through her eyes as he plodded after her. Taken another beating. Hang-dog, broken reed. His vacillation felt to him as though his eyes were rolling about in his head, his mouth drooling. He was surprised that passers-by did not stop and stare. Taking no notice of her, he plunged off in what he hoped was a westerly direction. She overtook him without effort and they walked quickly, abreast, with the earnest expressions of people who knew where they were going.

After a while he stopped and deliberately, without glancing at her, took the guide-book out of his pocket. He unfolded the map and studied it earnestly. He did not consult her. He then folded the map again, stacking it skilfully as a deck of cards, pocketed the guide-book and walked quickly on, now looking up and round as though seeking corroboration from the untraceable position of the sun. Out of the corner of her eye she saw dark shops, coral, gloves, lace and ivory. The question demanded at the beginning of the day began to haunt her again: what are we doing? Please God, what do we think we're doing? Her ankles had already begun to ache and swell. She fancied that when they had started out from the hotel, men had looked at her twice: and now, so quickly, they passed by as though she were invisible. She dared not search for her reflection in the dark windows – an unloved, unloving wife dressed (God knows, she thought, why I bother) in smart linen.

'Piazza di Spagna,' Bernard snapped triumphantly.

'Oh yes.' She congratulated him. 'So it is.'

'Look at the flowers, the umbrellas.'

'Yes. Aren't they pretty.'

'The British Consulate is here somewhere.'

'Is that where we're going?' She was faintly alarmed, concerned about the children left behind.

'Of course not. Why should we go to the Consulate?'

'I don't know. You seemed to make such a point of it.'

'I was simply telling you it is here.'

'Yes,' she said. 'All right. I see.'

They began to climb the steps. A girl and a boy approached them, coming down; wreathed together, they hovered on each step; their descent, since they gazed only at each other, seemed mesmerised. Bernard and Frances separated to pass them. When they moved together again they both looked sad and shy, knowing – as they so often did – that their thoughts were at that moment identical.

'A hundred and thirty-seven steps,' Bernard said, straightening his back, climbing more jauntily.

'Lincoln Cathedral has three hundred and sixty-five. One for each day of the year.'

'I didn't know you'd ever been to Lincoln.'

'Only once. When I was a child.'

'I'm surprised you remember so much about it. I thought you didn't like ancient monuments.'

She had fallen a little behind him. The headache from which she had suffered almost continually since they left England had flared up again. 'I like to be happy,' she said.

'Why the hell can't you be happy, then?'

'I was,' she said, suddenly defiant. 'When I was here before. I was happy.'

'Oh, for God's sake. So that's what you're mooning about.' He waited for her, noticing with terrible anger how heavily she climbed, how anxious her raised face with its powdered crevices and precisely coloured lips. 'I bring you away on a highly expensive holiday,' he said, 'and you behave like a child!'

'When we started – when we started out, it was a second honeymoon? When did it become a highly expensive holiday! Where?'

They faced each other, both trembling, on the graceful mellow steps. People running down, bounding up, glanced at them, noticing only a red-faced man and a well-dressed woman staring into each other's eyes.

They finished the climb in silence. She felt very weak, very frightened. Tenderness for him formed in her breast, her hands, her body. What could be done? 'The church . . .' she said, offering it to him, 'don't you want to . . .?'

He made a furious gesture, as though slapping down an importunate dog. Like a foolish dog, unwilling to be lost, she dodged along behind him. So swiftly, unexpectedly, everything was changed. Now it was she, feeling him dreadfully wronged, who longed to satisfy him; he who rejected her. Pride gave him a new appearance. He had become very pale, his skin greenish under the shadow of his haphazard shave.

'Where are we going?' she asked, breathless.

'Cook's.'

'But is this the way? Shall we take a taxi?'

He said quite kindly. 'There are plenty of taxis. Do exactly as you like.'

Encouraged by his tone – perhaps something could still be saved? – she said hesitantly, 'I'm dreadfully thirsty.'

He walked on for a few moments without answering. Would he even refuse to look after her? Then he sighed, and crossed the road. They were separated by the traffic and she believed, as she tried to make little rushes from the pavement, that he had shaken her off. But he was waiting at an iron table under a scalloped awning. She longed to refresh her face, but dreaded the *gabinetto*. Normally she would have powdered in front of him, stretched her lips for their coating of Love That Pink, sucked them in so that she looked briefly mouthless, an old woman. Now, for some reason, this was not possible. She sat limp, glistening, staring at the red ash-tray with its legend Fly TWA.

'Why do you want to go to Cook's?'

'You can fly home tomorrow.'

'Fly? Tomorrow? But—'

'You don't want to drive, do you? With *me*?'

'But . . .'

'Oh, shut up,' he said wearily.

She drank some of the cold beer. If things had really gone as far as this, nothing mattered. 'One thing, anyway. If we hadn't come, we'd never have known.'

He moved restlessly. 'Known what?'

'Is it' – she could hardly bear to use the word – 'hopeless?'

'You don't love me,' he said, with disgust. 'Of course it's hopeless.'

'Oh, *Bernard* . . .'

'I just like to get things straight, that's all.'

'I'm sorry.'

'So am I.'

'But we can't help—' she began. 'Growing old,' she was going to say, but could not manage it.

He waited, his hand clenched, staring at the unbecoming sandals he had bought for himself in Florence. A girl walked by with a poodle on a lead. His eyes flickered upwards. He turned abruptly, crouched over the table, hammering it softly with his clenched fist. 'Well? Well? What can't we help?'

'Nothing.' Like a sullen child with its mother's face on. Twisting, groping down to her heels, she managed to squeeze her shoes on again. She stood up uncertainly. 'We'd better go.'

This time they walked together. It was getting hot. The shops were full of pagoda bird-cages, confirmation dresses, gramophone records. The despair in Bernard was trying to break through. He could feel it threatening his eyes, his throat, the sturdy walls of his chest. He wheeled round into a narrow side street.

'Is this the way?' she asked, hurrying beside him.

He pulled the guide-book out of his pocket and shook it under her face. 'If you want to know the way,' he yelled quietly, 'look at the map, blast you! Look at the map!'

She ran a dozen steps in front of him and then, with a sort of hopeless dignity, began to walk. Perhaps he was not following her. Perhaps he had plunged off round some corner and was already lost. She made a great effort and forced herself almost to saunter up the long corridor of the street. There were no footsteps behind her. At last she stopped in front of a small, cheap clothes shop, staring fiercely at the shoddy cotton sweaters and poplin jeans, unthinkable for a woman like herself; tensing herself to look back, but too proud to do so. Her reflection, faceless, a dishevelled outline, glimmered in the window; she pushed distractedly at her hair, feeling the sweat on her forehead and her lips blenched, dried with heat and strain. Oh God, she cried to herself, it's so unfair, so *unfair*. Her face began to crumple, her mouth to square like a child's. Horrified at herself, she breathed quickly, intently concentrating on the goods in the window, the duster-yellow running into the tile-red and sky-blue and livid laurel-green.

'Frances . . .' Bernard said behind her – his tired, flat voice no longer angry.

Unthinking, on a sharp gasp of outrage (because he had followed her, or followed her too slowly? Because he had spoken, or not insisted on speaking more? Because he had seen her looking ugly or had not noticed?), she plunged into the shop, pulling the door shut behind her, stumbling down the unexpected stairs. The gloom, the smell of new, harsh cotton baffled her for a moment; she could not find the counter, was only aware that she was below street-level in a kind of haberdashers' tomb and that Bernard was peering down for her, waving his head slowly from side to side as he searched between the middy blouses and pantaloons.

'*Signora . . .?*'

'Oh!' she skipped, thoroughly flustered, up and round in the direction of the coaxing voice.

'The *Signora* wishes . . .?' The usual long, curving mouth set smiling round the usual scintillating teeth; the usual sober suit and the heavy ring on a stubby finger. All this, by sense rather than sight, she recognised immediately. Italians, like Asiatics and Africans, seemed to her exactly alike, distinguishable only by age and sex.

'Oh,' she said, 'yes. I wanted—' She looked wildly round the dark shop, swept over Bernard's remote aquarium face behind the high window, stopped short at a row of gingham skirts hanging in the gloom like flags in the remote corner of a cathedral. She hated gingham, unless it was used for other people's tablecloths, when she envied its simplicity. She detested full skirts, little-girl fashions, clothes for gadding and lounging. Nevertheless, she demanded breathlessly, 'A skirt – one of those gingham skirts. A blue one,' keeping her back resolutely turned to the window, forgetting that from the street the inside of the shop was invisible.

'Of course, madam.' The assistant's head circled with a curiously coy motion and stopped lop-sided on his neck, as though he were attempting to tuck it under a wing. 'And the waist . . .?'

'Twenty-four.' She lied automatically by two inches. 'Oh, I suppose it's centimetres. I don't know.' She glanced desperately towards the window. 'Just bring the skirt. I'll try it. Do you understand?'

'Naturally, madam, I understand. I was for some months in Scarborough.' He climbed, reached for the skirt, lowered it gently.

There was no one at the window and she suddenly realised that she might be abandoned, given up for lost.

'It's too small,' she wailed. 'I won't bother to try.'

'But you must try, madam . . .'

'No!'

'The waist of the *Signora* is that of a young girl.' He made it sound correct, gentle as a grammar-book phrase.

'But I don't want it!'

He slipped round the end of the counter, approached her softly. She was holding the skirt. He took it from her and held it against her body.

'The waist . . .' His hands grasped her firmly. 'The waist is perfect.'

'The skirt is too small,' she repeated stupidly.

'Pretty ...' he murmured. The skirt dropped to the floor, his hands slid two inches farther. He breathed rather loudly and edged forward, stepping on her toe.

My God, she thought, I'm being assaulted. She stared at his teeth and said very clearly, 'Please stop being so stupid.'

He smiled, apparently complimented.

'The *Signor*,' she said, her voice rising with panic, 'is in the street. The *Signor* is in the *strada*.'

He breathed over her. He was by no means brutal. There was, in fact, a kind of tired civility, almost generosity, as of someone graciously fulfilling her expectations.

'Stop it!' she rapped. 'Let me go!' And then, in a shrill, taut shout, 'Bernard? *Bernard?*'

The assistant hesitated for a moment. 'Bernard?' his troubled eyes seemed to ask, 'But that is not my name?' She twisted away from him, scrambled up the stairs, burst into the air, flung herself with sudden panting and sobbing (unexpected – she had not felt like weeping before), on the patient, gloomy bulk of her husband leaning against the wall and studying his map. Startled, he dropped the map, found himself restraining her.

'Didn't you hear me call? Didn't you hear?'

He shook his head in wonder.

'He made a pass at me!' she howled. 'He tried to—'

'In the shop? Who? The assistant?'

She nodded, shaking and sobbing inside his arm. A strand of hair was plastered across her forehead. Her face was hectic and ravaged by the sudden onslaught of tears. Gently, he replaced the strand of hair and offered his handkerchief. She took it, demanding wildly, 'Aren't you going to do something? Just stand there? Aren't you going to do anything?'

Her voice sounded so wild with grief that it penetrated, for the first time, the insensitive, protective covering of his heart. With awe and reluctance he heard himself saying, 'Well, it's your fault.'

'My . . .?' Sincerely bewildered, staring at him with wide, streaming eyes.

'You shouldn't be so attractive.' As with the words 'Eternal City' he longed to add, 'Driving men mad', but swallowed it back.

Her gaze, now humble, uncertain, did not leave his face. 'Don't be so silly . . .'

'I'm not,' he said painfully, 'being silly.'

Her eyes flickered, changed. He smiled a little.

'A happily married woman with two children!' Then he indulged himself, 'Driving men mad!'

'Oh!' She sobbed, nearly giggled, blew into the handkerchief. 'Oh, you are absurd!'

He glanced across the street. 'Come. We'd better move. We've attracted an audience.'

'Oh dear . . . Oh dear . . . Yes, we'd better go.'

'We'll get a taxi back to the hotel.'

'No . . .' She was submissive, trembling. 'No, we'll go to the Sistine Chapel.'

For a fraction of a second he hesitated. The temptation was very strong. Then, in his first moment of real perception, he knew that tomorrow the Sistine Chapel would still be there; and the day after; and for centuries. Whereas they, with such difficulty, such dragging steps, such pitiful reluctance, were approaching death.

'No,' he said, 'we'll go back to the hotel.'

He took her hand and led her away from the shop front. A little way up the street he put his arm around her and hitched her own round his broad waist. Before they had reached the end of it they had begun to run, laughing, stumbling like children in a three-legged race.

THE RENEGADE

They had finished their supper and were now sitting one each side of the fire in their comfortable, over-large armchairs. The standard lamp with the parchment shade was placed just behind Mrs Rachett's right shoulder, casting a brilliant, precise light on her knitting; her husband's Anglepoise did the same for his Lancelot Hogben, which was supported on a small, adjustable lectern so that the effort of reading was reduced to the movement of his small blue eyes darting from side to side under the overhanging cliffs of eyebrows. Between these two brilliances there was darkness; the room enclosed them, its low ceiling and thick curtains and beige colouring invisible. The fire, since Mrs Ratchett was economical and it was nearly nine o'clock, had stopped flaming. The dying coals were topped by a

small, damp log which hissed and crumbled on its under-
side into grey ash. The hissing of the log and the nibbling
of steel knitting needles sounded as though they were
competing against a lifelong silence.

They were both in their middle fifties. He read as she
knitted, for occupation, but without the same tangible
result. Her thoughts, as she lifted her arms and pulled
more wool off the ball, were livelier, wider in their scope.
His, as his eyes darted from row to row of print, were
concentrated on the throbbing wound of loneliness and
boredom situated somewhere in the region of his larynx.
It was a constriction, a gathering of the walls of his throat
into a severe pain which stretched up on either side of his
head, through the intricate passages of his ears into the
caves of his mind. So, exploring it, he imagined. Poisoned
with loneliness. Dying of loneliness. He was, he knew, at
his last gasp.

However, this agony was no longer new to him. He
had lived with it for years. His eyes beetled across the
pages, his small feet were planted squarely on the beige
rug in order that the short legs might support the weight
of his stomach. His stubby forefinger and thumb held the
page ready for turning, conscious that in the future this, at
least, would be necessary. His pipe hung loosely from his
mouth. When he slept, as he would from time to time, his
pipe fell on to his chest and woke him up. His pullover was
patterned with small darns in varying shades of grey.

'They took Mr Dodge to hospital,' his wife said suddenly, heaving wool.

His eyes stopped, shot upwards. 'Who?'

'Jack Dodge. They think it's gallstones.' The needles raced in and out. She kept her elbows pressed to her sides although there was plenty of room in the chair for two women of her size.

'I can't see him tomorrow,' her husband said angrily.

'It wouldn't take long, dear.'

'It would take the whole morning.'

'The buses are so awkward for Mrs Dodge. You could take her in to the hospital.'

She was pleading with him, in a brisk voice, never stopping her knitting. He knew this and it sickened him. It was not that she cared about the Dodges any more than he did; but she cared desperately what they thought of him. She longed for people to say how good the Vicar is, how kind; to throw open the Vicarage for orgies of calves-foot jelly and whist, to trot about with little baskets, to feel that he glowed like a human benediction over her clinics and Mothers' Union meetings and Jumble Sales. Was he born for this? The question obsessed him, particularly towards the end of the week when Sunday's sermon was not yet released. Friday evenings are always difficult, Mrs Ratchett would like to have said, as though fondly excusing him. There was no one to say it to, and in any case it would have been another lie. All evenings are difficult, he wanted to shout, and Friday is the worst. Was there no truth in the world?

'I suppose,' he said, 'the Dodges are more important than my sermon? You don't care about the agonies I go through, I perfectly realise that.'

She did not answer, implying that of course the Dodges were more important than his sermon. He did not know any words bad enough to express how he felt. He was alone in a desert of futility. He would have plunged his head into his hands shouting, 'Oh God, oh God, why hast thou forsaken me?' if he didn't know that afterwards, while he waited behind his rigid fingers, he would hear nothing but the tapping of knitting needles. Was there no outrage or excess he could commit which would prove to her, prove to her – what? Exhausted, he slumped behind his book again.

'Pat used to play with the little Dodge girl,' his wife said quietly.

He grunted. It was unlike Helen to be so remorseless. Acceptance of defeat was part of her philosophy. It is no use, she would say gently, kicking against the pricks; it is no use, Brian, beating your head against a brick wall. So what was she up to, nagging him like this? With difficulty, heaving himself backwards, he inserted his finger and thumb into his watch pocket and pulled out a gold Albert. Nearly time for the News. He pushed the lectern away and lumbered to his feet, a short, very heavy man with a large head stuck well down and forward on his shoulders so that even his slow, almost motionless walk – the feet moved, but the big body remained obstinately static, like a weight inched forward on tiny castors – seemed like a slow charge.

'Pat was very fond of her,' his wife said, with what seemed to him a kind of recklessness.

'Pat loves everyone. She's generous, she's got a warm heart. Pat is like me – she's in love with the whole word!' This statement was delivered with genuine passion. It finished the business of the Dodges, reduced Helen to her usual indrawn silence, her face gathered tightly round a vanished mouth. The radio blared out with a depression approaching from Iceland. The rounded, indifferent tones of the announcer goaded Ratchett into a moment's madness. 'Fools!' he shouted. But he did not, as intended, turn the radio off. He simply turned it down and went back to his chair. His wife was threading a number of stitches on to a large safety-pin. He closed his eyes and immediately looked twenty years older.

While the News worked steadily through from the international situation to the football scores both the Ratchetts, in their different ways, thought about their daughter. Patricia was thirteen and at a boarding-school for the daughters of clergy, fifteen miles away. They both shared this starting point for their thoughts, although Ratchett had left it long before his wife and was transformed by feeling while she was still wondering whether the Matron really saw that they changed their underclothes . . . Pat and I, Ratchett thought. My only friend. My little sweetheart. He didn't exactly miss her, but he thought how he would write one of his letters telling her how he missed her. You and I, he would say, are just the same, we belong together, don't take any notice of those bone-headed fools who try to lick you into shape. Be free, my darling, free and proud as a beautiful bird . . . What are we going to do about her, his wife thought. Perhaps they will manage to control her, but oh dear, those terrible tantrums and so untidy with it. Her normally bewildered expression became more pronounced. She struggled with her knitting through a sudden fog of tears. Everything passes, she insisted, fumbling for help. Her husband had destroyed her faith in God in the process of destroying his own. She was thrown back on proverbs burned into wood and hung on her bedroom wall: so many gods, so many creeds, so many paths that wind and wind, while just the art of being kind is all the sad world needs. Thinking of Patricia could always induce in her great unhappiness, guilt, a knowledge of failure. She suspected that kindness was not what Pat needed at all, but a firm hand. She loved her with deep, inarticulate devotion. She would do anything for her, but apart from continually supplying her with warm knickers and treacle toffee there never seemed much she could do. She felt dreadfully tired and at last stabbed the needles into the ball of wool, furled the knitting round it like a flag, tucked it into her embroidered knitting bag and sat back with her hands clasped, her eyes closed, shrunken to the size of a child.

Directly with no apparent hesitation, the little girl marched to the centre of the cross-roads where two policemen, their oilskin capes shining under a street lamp, were standing together in slovenly attitudes, just about to go off duty. The cinema was closed, the streets empty. Because of the street lights there seemed to be less fog in the town. She had already walked two miles. She was still too excited to feel tired, but she was damp with fog, her straight hair clamped to her head, her nose wet, her steel-rimmed glasses giving her a strange, rakish appearance.

She reached the policemen and said, 'Excuse me. Could you tell me the way to Blicksley?'

They were very tall, their domed helmets leaning towards her under the light. They saw a small, square child in a blue shirt, no coat, a serge skirt and thick, wrinkled stockings. They seemed to ponder her reluctantly.

'Blicksley?' one of them asked. She nodded. They turned to each other, creaking in their oilskins. 'That's on the Derby road.'

'About thirteen miles,' the other one said slowly.

'Thank you.' She looked between them, up a narrow street that became, as it wound higher, obliterated in fog. 'Is that it?'

They turned, looked at the street, nodded.

'Thank you,' she said again. 'Good night.'

'Just a minute,' the younger of the two policemen looked at her unwillingly. 'Anything wrong, miss?'

'Nothing at all,' she said carelessly, moving off.

'You're not walking to Blicksley at this time of night?'

'Oh no,' she grinned quickly, edging away from them. 'My uncle lives on the Blicksley road, that's all. My bicycle broke down. That's why I'm walking.'

'What's your name?' trying not to sound suspicious.

'Ann Barry.' This was true. Her name was Patricia Ann Barry Ratchett.

'You know a Barry on the Blicksley road?' the young one asked the other one uncomfortably.

'My uncle's name isn't Barry. It's Dodge. Thank you very much. Good night.' She ran across the road and didn't stop running until she was half-way up the street. Then, out of breath, her heart jumping, she looked over her shoulder. The cross-roads were empty. The fog streamed down the hill and beyond a tall bridge she could see the last of the street lamps.

After ten minutes of the Pastorale Symphony, relayed at full volume, Mrs Ratchett opened her eyes, pulled herself to her feet and prepared to go to bed. This involved going into the bitterly cold kitchen and making a cup of cocoa for her husband, a hot-water bottle for herself. She returned to the sitting-room with the bottle burning her arm and the cocoa slopping over into the saucer. Ominously, the radio had been turned off and he was sitting with his head in his hands. She put the cocoa down as quietly as possible and tried to tiptoe away. There were many times in her daily life when, out of pure will-power, she almost achieved invisibility.

'How long do you think I can carry on like this?' he groaned. He had timed her creep to the door exactly. She took a deep breath.

'We all have to carry on to the end, don't we?' she said brightly, stretching out her hand to the doorknob.

'If it weren't for you and Pat,' he said, 'I should throw up the whole thing tomorrow.'

She had heard this countless times before. She said at random, 'When you have turned your hand to the plough . . .' and seized the doorknob.

'I must get away,' he shouted softly, pummelling his large forehead with his fists.

'There's the Rotary Conference in April. You always,' she lied desperately, 'enjoy that.'

'Pah!' The explosion shot him out his chair, landed him standing in front of the dead fire with his face shaking. 'My God, Helen, why have you got so little imagination?'

'I'm sorry,' she said, sounding humble, turning the doorknob very slightly.

'I have made up my mind. Tomorrow I am going to write to the Nature Colony at Eastbourne. I shall book a chalet for myself and Patricia. After Easter, naturally.' As he said this, he decided on it. The constriction in his throat vanished. He challenged her, his blazing little eyes ferreting her out in the darkness.

'The Nature Colony?' she asked faintly. 'But aren't they all' – she almost whispered the word – 'nude?'

'Naked,' he said triumphantly.

Her face had flushed deeply, not from modesty, but from unhappiness. She clung to the door, a lifetime of effort crumbling under her feet. 'But what shall we tell the parish? What will people say?'

'Ha!' Without moving, he seemed to pounce on her, drag her back into the room again. His voice, which could fill a large church without effort, was at its most resonant; his eyes whirled and crackled like small Catherine-wheels. 'What will people say?' he echoed. 'What will people say? Do you imagine I care? Does Patricia care? Don't you glory in the thought of the child running and playing in the free air, her body golden in the sunlight, untrammelled, liberated? Have you no feeling, none at all, for the simple things of life, the great, glorious freedom . . .'

He went on and on. At the picture of Patricia running about naked – the child had a weak chest – Mrs Rachett had begun to feel sick. She stood, growing smaller and smaller, clutching her hot-water bottle and telling herself everything passes, everything passes. Finally, hearing nothing but his loud breathing, she looked up.

'I don't know what they will think at St Mary's,' she said timidly.

'St Mary's! A crowd of frustrated spinsters! Do you think Patricia cares about them?'

'You sent her there, dear. It's her sixth school, you know. I do think you should consider—'

'I consider the truth,' he said. The outburst over, he felt the nagging constriction again, the desire to yawn. Looking down at his great stomach he suddenly visualised it naked, exposed. 'You'd better go to bed,' he said bleakly. 'Nothing will ever make you understand.'

She bowed, assenting, and began to creep out of the room.

'Whoever changed the altar cloth,' he said peevishly, 'put the frontal on inside out.'

She heard him, but did not answer. As she closed the door and started slowly up the stairs she found herself wondering what does it matter if the frontal is inside out, what does it matter.

'Actually,' Patricia said, 'I've run away.' She held her mug of coffee in both hands, letting the steam melt the end of her nose.

'From home?' the lorry driver asked mildly. He had picked her up on the loneliest stretch of the moor, crying bitterly and half frozen. He was about eighteen and his lorry shook with a terribly, tinny palsy. At first she had been overwhelmed with gratitude, but now she was glad to be out of it for a while. The narrow room, really no more than a shed, was warm, everything clouded with steam. Even the Pepsi-Cola advertisements were corrugated with damp and the ham sandwiches tasted like wet flannel.

'Of course not,' she said, blowing upwards at a moustache of bubbles. 'From school.'

'Uh-huh.' He gulped his coffee, eyeing the tired woman knitting behind the tea-urn. 'And what's your mum and dad going to say to that?'

'Oh, they won't say anything. At least, Mummy might. But Daddy won't. He's the one who counts.'

He nodded absently. As far as he understood, this was how it should be. He was too young to take kids seriously, particularly kids like this one. The woman looked at him and yawned enormously. Poor old bag, he thought, and let his mouth fall open, the cigarette stuck to his lower lip.

'You don't have to worry,' the child said. 'I mean, as far as Daddy's concerned you're doing absolutely the right thing. He'd be awfully grateful to you for giving me a lift. I mean, you know, he won't be angry or anything.'

'Who is your dad, anyway?' he asked. From the way she talked he might be the Chief Constable or God or something.

'He's the Vicar of Blicksley,' she said proudly; then, dismayed by his blank look, she added hurriedly, 'But he's not a bit like a vicar, he doesn't even wear his dog-collar except on Sundays. I bet he'll be glad to see me.' The boy stared at her, the cigarette burning into long ash on his lip. 'Look,' she said eagerly, feeling he was unconvinced, 'I've got a letter from him here . . .'

The boy's eyes followed her movements as she dug in the pocket of her skirt and produced first a grubby hand-kerchief, then two gritty pieces of chewing gum, then a sheet of paper folded very small. 'Shall I read it to you?' she asked eagerly. He shrugged, flicking the brown ciga-rette stub on to the floor.

'*My darling Pat,*' she read, smoothing the paper and taking a great bite of sandwich, '*How lovely to hear from you . . .* Oh well, that part doesn't matter.' She munched urgently, turning the paper over. 'This is the bit. *I understand you so well, my little bird. If there is ever anything I can do to help you, you know you have only to ask. It is my sole desire to see you soar above the pettiness, the crass stupidity of our so-called intelligent society. Bless you, my pet, and may no one ever clip your wings . . .*'

She looked up, her dark eyes squinting wildly. 'So you see, it's quite all right about me running away. You've no idea what St Mary's is like. You just have no idea.'

'Do they beat you?' he asked, with slight interest.

'No. I'd sooner they did. They just murder us by slow degrees.' Crouching with her little square hands grasping the mug, her bright eyes squinting over its rim, her hair now fine and dry and wild as feathers, she made him uneasy.

'Come off it,' he said. 'You're imagining things.'

'Oh no, I'm not. D'you know, the term's only been going five weeks and do you know how many conduct marks I've got? Four. If you get three in one term they expel you. I got my fourth tonight. That's why I ran away. After all, I don't see what the difference is, do you?'

'Come on,' he said. 'Let's get going. I'd just like to see your dad's face when you get there, that's all.'

She got up slowly. As she trailed out after him the woman behind the tea-urn smiled and said, 'Good night, love.' It was peculiar, but Patricia suddenly had the feeling that this was the place she should have stopped at. It was good enough, so hot and bright and steamy; a place of her own, where her parents, her friends, her school-teachers had never been.

She hesitated at the door. 'Good night,' she said. 'Perhaps I'll come here again one day.'

The woman looked at her stupidly. Like everyone else, she didn't understand.

● ● ●

Mr Ratchett made up the boiler and wound the grandfather clock. His eyes were dead, hooded at the end of a day in which nothing more could happen. He had done practically nothing since he got up at six o'clock that morning except eat and sleep, and yet he was tired out.

The thought of tomorrow, which he would spend at his desk, filled him with apprehension. No intelligent man, he would say, could be expected to think of a new sermon once a week. But he tried. Every week he tried, struggling to catch something, some blazing truth, which had never been caught before; running, with that clumsy, blind, eager spirit of his into every cul-de-sac, every morass and obstruction in the history of knowledge, pouncing on dead hopes and carrying them tenderly until, with horror, he felt them disintegrate in his arms. His text hardly mattered, and this week he had decided on an old one: Suffer the little children to come unto me, for such is the Kingdom of Heaven. He had interpreted it in a dozen ways before, but this week it would be the conflict of innocence and authority, the emancipation of the spirit into a society ruled by love alone, a society in which the Church, marriage, politics, money, were no longer necessary but everyone gambolled naked and unashamed in a balmy Elysium, a spiritual Eastbourne, Paradise. All this, as he carried his early morning tea-tray into his study, filled the electric kettle, tidily replaced Lancelet Hogben in the bookshelf, elated him. He was almost happy. He had at last forgotten

Mrs Dodge and her ridiculous difficulty with the buses. When the front doorbell rang he swung round on his small feet, abruptly reduced to terrible anger.

Fools, he thought. Fools. Why can't they leave me alone? Some old idiot dying, dead, what am I supposed to do about it? He charged, impelled by fury, down the hall, into the porch, unbolted the heavy door and flung it open. The fog poured in as though through a sluice gate.

'Hallo,' Patricia said, and stepped inside.

She had planned the whole thing. He would be surprised at first, of course. That was why, in spite of the fact that all she wanted to do was to run to him and fling her arms round his neck, she had to behave as though everything was perfectly normal. Afterwards, when he had got over the shock, she could let herself go – the terror and the tiredness, the unfairness, the fact that she had wanted, really wanted to be good, the dreadful things they had done to her ... He would rock her on his knee and finally tuck her up in bed in her own warm room. After that he would come down and ring up Miss Fairweather and probably – the picture had got a little confused here – challenge her to a duel. So, hardly looking at him, she walked straight past him into the sitting-room. It was a shock to find the lights switched off and the fire out. Before she had found the switch he had come pelting after her. He suddenly looked quite small, much smaller and older than she had remembered.

'Patricia!' he gobbled. 'What—?'

'I've run away,' she said shakily. She wanted, more than anything else, to cry.

'Be quiet, be quiet,' he hissed. 'Don't let your mother hear.' He closed the door and switched on the light. He seemed to be out of breath. 'Run away? Run away?'

She nodded and began to cry, her whole small, solid body shaking. The pale centre light illuminated the room like a deserted stage, stripping it of all its mystery and comfort. She noticed her mother's knitting bag hanging on the back of the chair and the thought that her mother had been sitting here innocently knitting while she herself was making such a terrible journey started a new, uncontrollable wail of grief.

'*Will* you be quiet?' he demanded, beside himself. 'If your mother should hear of this—!'

Her mother would know before long anyway, Patricia thought. She didn't understand. She and her father always had a sort of conspiracy against her mother. Her mother was like everyone else. They were so different. What was he so anxious about? The tears poured scalding hot down her cold cheeks. She groped for her handkerchief but could only find his letter, which she stuffed back into her pocket again.

'Hanky?' she sobbed desolately. He gave her one and she blew her nose. The noise made him wince.

'Now,' he said, 'you'd better sit down and tell me what on earth this is all about.'

This was what she had thought he would say, but it sounded quite different. She sat down on her mother's foot-stool and he sat on an upright chair at a slight distance, anxiously fumbling for a cigarette. His hand, as he flicked and flicked again at his lighter, was trembling.

'First,' he said in a sharp, stage whisper, 'who knows about this?'

'Nobody,' she stammered. 'I mean, nobody except—'

'Except who?'

'Well, I got a lift on a lorry, the driver was awfully nice, he gave me some coffee at a place—'

'A place? What place? Not in Blicksley?'

'Oh no. Miles away.'

'Thank God for that. I hope you didn't tell him who you were, this driver?'

She nodded, her breath coming in little shivers.

'You told him you had run away from school?' he asked, with a kind of muted scream.

She nodded again.

He got up and began to pace about. At last he sat down in his own armchair and she could feel that some fierce struggle was finished, something had been overcome. She looked up at him, eyes and nose dumbly streaming. Awkwardly, with a curious feeling of distaste, he patted her shoulder.

'Well,' he said, 'you'd better tell me the whole story.'

She began at the beginning, or what she thought was the beginning. She had gone back to school meaning, really

240

meaning to be good. Then one day she had thrown her Latin grammar across the room just as Miss Bateman came through the door and it had hit Miss Bateman and broken her glasses and after that she had been found talking to the gardener's boy and after that she had lost her prayer-book and they said she was lying and then this evening she slid down the banisters and they said she'd answered back, so she said, 'Well, my father says you're all a lot of frustrated old spinsters so I don't care, and why shouldn't I answer back if I want to?' And after that she had been sent to bed.

Her father had closed his eyes. The lids flickered but the rest of his face, sagging as it did when he took his teeth out, was expressionless. She was bitterly cold and crouched nearer his legs for warmth.

'So then I thought I'd run away, because they'd be bound to expel me anyway. So I got dressed under the bed-clothes and put on my dressing-gown and then when they'd put the lights out I pretended I wanted to go to the lav and I left my dressing-gown in the lav and climbed out of the window and down the fire-escape and . . .'

He opened his eyes. 'But your dormitory is on the top floor. You might have been killed!'

'I suppose so,' she said simply.

'Go on,' he muttered. Vicar's Daughter Falls To Her Death. He felt his hands sweating.

'Well, that's all really.' It was by no means all, but she was so exhausted, so cold, that the rest of the story didn't seem to matter. Nothing mattered except the fact that she would soon be in bed, her mother would get up and make her a hot-water bottle, hot milk, kiss her good night, tell her that they would talk about it tomorrow. Nothing had gone quite right, but tomorrow it would be different. Her teeth had begun chattering again. 'Please,' she whimpered, 'please can I go to bed now?'

'To bed?' His eyes were switched on again with sudden brilliance. 'To bed? Good heavens, child, of course you can't go to bed!' He got up, carelessly pushing her away from him. 'Come along,' he said. 'You'd better wear your mother's gardening coat, it's hanging in the hall.'

'Why?' she breathed.

'Why?' As he turned on her, his whole face quivering, purple with suppressed outrage, she stepped back, her mouth dropping open as though she had already been struck. 'Why?' he yelled quietly. 'Do you realise what you have done? Did you think for one moment of your mother, of me, of my position in the parish? Do you realise that at this minute they may be scouring the countryside for you, that it may get into the papers? What do you think people will say? How am I supposed to talk to those boys and girls at the Youth Club when my own daughter—!' The telephone rang and he charged at it, controlling himself as he lifted the receiver and saying in reassuring, well-modified tones, 'Blicksley two-one-five?'

A shrill, distant cackle began. He cut it short with dignity. 'Yes, Miss Fairweather, she is here with me now.

I am bringing her back immediately. Naturally. I think I have made her see the gravity ... I quite agree with you, of course ... In about half an hour, then ... I can't tell you how sorry I am ...' He put the receiver down gently. When Patricia looked up again, with as much difficulty as though her neck were broken, he was standing holding her mother's gardening coat open in front of him. Without a word she went to him, turned her back so that he could heave it over her shoulders. She followed him out of the door, the hem of the coat trailing along the ground behind her.

She sat through the whole of the journey numb, bludgeoned with misery. Her father drove with the recklessness common to many clergymen, as though death were something to be met half-way. As they swerved over the cross-roads where the two policemen had told her the way, he suddenly blurted out, 'I don't want you to think I am angry with you, Patricia.'

She said nothing.

'I am desperately hurt,' he said. 'But I am not angry.'

She moved inside the coat, the feeble, pointless movement of something that has just been born.

'I realise,' he said, 'that you were not quite yourself when you decided on this – escapade.'

The prolonged silence made him uneasy. He gripped the wheel as though to wrench it out of the steering column.

'You may have misunderstood,' he said, 'not fully grasped the meaning – Perhaps I have been mistaken in talking to you as though you were . . .' His voice, usually so definite, trailed away. He picked it up again with an effort. 'We all have to learn to toe the line,' he said flatly.

They turned in at the drive gates, the headlamps shining on wet laurel and privet.

'Can't you say something?' he shouted.

The car drew up in front of the enormous, gaunt building. Behind the glass door, waiting in a quiet dressing-gown and her hair just snatched out of curlers, stood Miss Fairweather. She opened the door as Patricia climbed slowly up the steps. Patricia walked through the door and stood in the hall without moving, swamped in the brown overcoat of her small mother. Mr Rachett came in with a bustle. The door closed and Patricia heard Miss Fairweather say, 'Emily, will you put Patricia straight to bed? The guest room, as you know.'

Suddenly, like someone delivered to the firing squad and at last believing it, the child turned and threw herself on her father, pummelling his shoulders, clinging to his lapels so that she was lifted off her feet as he moved backwards, trying to shake her off.

'Don't let them!' she screamed. 'Take me back with you, don't leave me here, don't leave me, please, please, please! Daddy, don't let them!'

'Now, Patricia,' Miss Fairweather said. 'Now, Patricia . . .'

'I won't go!' she howled. 'I won't! I want Daddy, I want to go home, I want Daddy!'

'Control yourself!' Mr Ratchett shouted. 'Control yourself!'

She slumped against him, shivering. He could have picked her up in one hand. He stood with his arms by his sides, petrified.

'If you're a good girl,' Miss Fairweather said briskly, 'you shall see your father before he goes. Now go with Emily. Your father will come and see you.'

'Do you promise?'

Miss Fairweather's lips tightened. 'Of course.'

'Do you promise?' the child demanded, turning to her father.

He nodded stiffly.

'Cross your – cross your heart?'

'Yes, yes. Now do as you're told and go to bed.'

She allowed herself to be led up the front stairs, not even noticing this rare privilege, and along the interminable corridors to the cold, chintzy guest room overlooking the drive. Emily, one of the maids, undressed her without speaking, buttoned her into her pyjamas and watched her creep into bed.

'You're a fine one,' she said. 'Whatever made you go and do a thing like that?'

'Don't turn the light off. My father's coming.'

'He can turn it on again when he comes.' Emily switched the light off and shut the door. Her footsteps slapped away up the corridor.

When he comes, Patricia thought, I'll say I'm sorry. She was shuddering uncontrollably and curled up with her knees on her chest, her arms wrapped tightly round them, to keep herself still, to comfort herself.

'So long as people don't think,' Mr Ratchett said, 'that I encouraged the child in any way. You must understand that I am as deeply disturbed by this as you are, Miss Fairweather.'

'I am sure,' Miss Fairweather said, 'that people will realise that neither you nor the school are to blame. Patricia has a very strong will of her own. We have to curb it, Mr Ratchett.'

She was edging him towards the front door. He had found their talk, among all those crucifixes and water-colours, a tremendous strain, not helped by the fact that even in her dressing-gown, as a symbol of authority she terrified him.

'I quite agree,' he mumbled. 'So right. There is just one more thing. I did say something about seeing her—'

'Patricia will be much better left to sleep,' Miss Fairweather said firmly. 'Too much emotion can have far-reaching effects on girls of her age. We must think of Patricia as suffering from a slight illness, an indisposition, Mr Ratchett. I assure you she is in good hands.'

'I'm very grateful to you,' he muttered. 'Very grateful indeed.'

The door closed, the bolt shot across, the light snapped out. In the darkness he hurried down the steps, bundled into the small car, slammed the door and switched on the headlamps. What a relief, he thought, as he started up the engine. My God – it was almost a prayer – what a relief. The car shot round the gravel crescent, headed towards home. He looked back once, gripped with a moment's uneasiness. The blur in an upstairs window might possibly have been a child, but the cry thrown out to him was soundless and hardly misted the glass. He drove on, vindicated. In some vaguely disquieting way he no longer felt lonely. People would say he had done the right thing, and as for Patricia . . . Everything passes, he told himself, settling more comfortably into his seat. Everything passes.

WHAT A LOVELY SURPRISE

Paul Lawrence came back from work early. Jill lost count of the pile of shirts she was checking and impatiently started again, cramming each shirt into the laundry basket and muttering: 'One . . . two . . . three . . . four . . .' By the time she had captured them all and written them down in the book, he had shouted for the children and, after a great deal of rustling and whispering, they had shut themselves in the sitting-room.

With desperate speed, she began to count sheets. Louisa, their twelve-year-old daughter, came two steps at a time up the stairs, stopped short on the landing and said furiously, 'Oh. There you are. Can't you move?'

'But I'm in the middle of doing the laundry.'

'Well, we've got to bring something upstairs. Can't you just go away for a minute?'

Jill dropped her armful of sheets; she had already forgotten how many there were. 'All right,' she said, trying to look pleased. 'I suppose so.'

She went and sat on her bed. She was tired, and there was nothing to do in the bedroom so she just sat on the bed and waited. In a few moments she heard them coming up the stairs, the crackle of new, stiff brown paper, her husband swearing as he stumbled over the laundry basket.

'Where shall we put them?'

'Up in the attic, stupid.'

'Won't she go up to the attic?'

'Of course she won't.'

'Well how do you know she won't?'

'Oh, do be *quiet* . . .'

They creaked on up the stairs. She gave them another couple of minutes, then crept out of the bedroom and began counting the sheets again.

Paul came down from the attic hitting the dust off his suit and looking exhausted.

'Hallo,' he said. 'What on earth are you doing?'

'I should have thought it was obvious,' she said, writing down six sheets.

'Isn't it rather a peculiar time to be doing the laundry?'

'Well, it goes tomorrow.'

'Oh. I see.'

He realised, of course, that she couldn't do the laundry tomorrow. He sat down heavily on the stairs, watching her.

'There's an awful lot of it,' he said gloomily. 'Couldn't we cut down on it a bit?'

She realised that he had spent too much money today and was regretting it. She scooped up three pairs of his pyjamas and pushed them into the corners of the basket.

'If you'd wear drip-dry shirts,' she said, 'like everyone else.'

'But I loathe all that nylon and terylene and stuff.'

'Well, then. Eight shirts at one and seven pence each. Pyjamas are one and ten. No one else sends any clothes to the laundry. Why don't you buy a washing machine?' At last she had the whole lot battened down. She straightened herself, pushing the hair out of her eyes. 'You could have bought me one for my birthday, come to think of it.'

He was alarmed. 'Really? Would you have liked a washing machine? I didn't think of it.'

'No,' she said. 'I wouldn't.'

'I could have got one on the H.P.,' he insisted. 'But I didn't think of it.'

'But I don't want one!' she said, smiling desperately.

'All right, then why did you say—?'

The children came out of the attic and peered down over the banisters. 'Are you going to stay there all night?' Louisa asked. 'We want to bring something down.'

'All right,' Jill said, dragging the laundry basket across the landing and bumping it down the stairs. 'I'm just going.'

She had prepared, as far as possible, for tomorrow. Her birthday cake, with one deceitful candle, was ready in the larder; she had washed the kitchen floor and bought groceries for two days and checked that the tin opener and the corkscrew were both in the drawer. She took a pile of mending and sat down on the window-seat in the sitting-room. The sun was misty, the small, narrow gardens littered with disorderly September flowers, leaning stacks of Michaelmas daisies, chrysanthemums like spilled copper, Aaron's rod and seedy willow-herb, slovenly splashes of dahlia against the grey brick walls. Somewhere somebody was already burning leaves. The clock in the hall chimed and struck the hour.

As she counted the strokes, one hand gloved in her husband's sock, she was momentarily caught by a sharp, composite memory of all her birthdays. She could actually feel anticipation, even pleasure, flash through her, as though tomorrow really contained a mystery; as though she might unwrap something – a doll, the shrouded bulk of a new bicycle – which would really be a surprise, an astonishing happiness. It had left her before the clock had finished striking. If only, she thought, stabbing the hard heel of the sock with the needle, it was all over.

'We want the scissors,' Jane announced, bursting through the door. Her round, seven-year-old face was stern. 'We are very busy.'

'Bring them back,' Jill said. 'And be careful.'

The door slammed, the child pounded upstairs. Two minutes later she was back again.

'Where's the string?'

'I don't think,' Jill said brightly, 'we've got any string.'

Dismay threatened. 'What shall we do, then?'

Jill pulled her hand out of the sock, lifted the pile of mending off her knee and began to look for the string. She groped in the back of shelves, hunted through the drawer of the desk which contained bits of sealing-wax, dried-up bottles of marking ink, three or four unidentified keys, two pipes, various bits of broken china, an old toothbrush and some lighter flints, but no string. Jane sat down patiently and looked at a magazine. Jill looked systematically through the broom cupboard and kitchen drawers and produced at last a roll of green garden twine and six yards of new pink ribbon intended for reviving someone's party dress. 'You'll have to manage with this,' she said.

Jane looked at it critically. 'All right,' she said. 'I suppose it'll do.'

She went off, and Jill sat down again, lifting back the mending. She decided not to bother with the sock, but to do something restful, like changing all the buttons on Louisa's overcoat. They hadn't brought back the scissors, so she gnawed and pulled at the buttons for a while and then gave up, folding the overcoat neatly over the back of the chair and waiting.

Becky, the middle one, was the next to come down. She put her sharp little face, weighted with horn-rimmed glasses and topped with a scrub of chopped red hair, round the door and asked, 'Daddy says, where's the glue?'

'There might be some in the cupboard.'

Becky was ten and had just finished a two-year-long impersonation of Roy Rogers. The change had been sudden and extreme. The checked shirt, the patched jeans, the stringy neck scarf were still in a heap on her bedroom floor. She now wore one of Louisa's petticoats trailing its grubby frill two inches below a velvet skirt she had salvaged from the dressing-up box. She also wore ballet pumps and a large broderie Anglaise blouse which Jill remembered putting away to give, in another three or four years' time, to Louisa. Round her neck, instead of the scarf, she wore a broken necklace of plastic beads, cunningly mended with fuse wire. She looked as though she had just been converted by a visiting missionary.

'Becky—' Jill began.

'Yes?' The huge spectacles, which the child had mistakenly been allowed to choose for herself, flashed innocently.

'Oh, nothing. It should be in the bottom shelf.'

'I've got it. By the way, how old will you be tomorrow?'

'A hundred and ninety-five.'

'No. Really.'

'Thirty-nine.' But she couldn't help adding, 'I think.'

'Gosh. Daddy didn't know.' She wandered to the door.

'I asked him,' she explained. 'He said oh, about thirty-five or something.'

Jill smiled. Her face was already beginning to ache a little.

'We need to know, you see, for the play.'

'Do you mean to say there's going to be a play?' There was always a play. It took up, mercifully in some ways, most of the afternoon. 'Really?' she asked incredulously.

'Perhaps I shouldn't have told you. Oh dear.'

'It's all right. I'll just pretend I don't know.'

In a little while her husband came down.

'Well,' he asked in a distraught way, 'and how's the birthday girl?'

She looked at him imploringly. She had the absurd idea that she could ask him to abandon the whole thing.

'The children are working like blacks,' he said.

'How sweet of them.' She smiled quickly.

'Looking forward to your day off?'

'Oh yes. Of course I am.'

'That's good.'

He settled himself in an armchair and closed his eyes. The expression on his face was that of a man doggedly resting before a battle that might well be his last.

Next morning she woke, opened her eyes, took in the grey square of window and the sound of rain, snapped her eyes shut again. Thirty-nine, she thought. It didn't mean anything. She was relieved and, turning cautiously over, settled to sleep again.

In five minutes the alarum began to ring. Her husband had, of course, taken the day off. However, being her birthday, the alarum rang half an hour earlier than usual. He groaned and humped about the bed a little, then got up. She heard him putting on his dressing-gown and shuffling out of the room.

'Honestly,' she heard before the door closed, 'we've been up for *hours* . . .'

She got quickly out of bed and brushed her hair, peering at herself in the damp mirror with the superstitious feeling that overnight her hair should have gone grey, the wrinkles multiplied. However, she looked much the same, except for the anxious smile that already seemed to be driven into her face. She shut the window and switched on the fire, then got back into bed and folded her hands calmly over her stomach. The great thing, she told herself, is to relax. Just relax, and it may all be quite painless.

The door opened and the three clear, sturdy voices struck up:

'Happy Birthday to you,

Happy Birthday to you,

Happy Birthday' – Paul joined in rather haphazardly – 'dear Mother,

Happy Birthday to you!'

'Oh,' she said. 'What a lovely surprise.'

They filed in, business-like, serious, dumped their packages on the bed, kissed her and stood back. Paul followed with the tea-tray and kissed her and wished her a happy birthday.

'Well,' she said. 'I don't know where to start.'

They glanced at each other and giggled shortly. She began untying the pink ribbon.

'Oh,' she said, 'what a beautiful card! Did you make it, Becky?'

Becky nodded. 'I made up the poem too.'

'Let's read it, then.

"Thirty-nine is not such a very great age to be

Think how you'd feel if today you were ninety-three."'

There was a moment's silence.

'Well,' Jill said, 'I think it's perfectly lovely. And a blotter, too! Just what I wanted. *Thank* you, darling.' She kissed Becky, who blushed almost purple.

'Open mine now,' Jane said.

'But it's a needle case! And you made it all by yourself! *Thank* you, darling.'

While Jill was kissing Jane, Louisa, who thought her youngest sister a frightful show-off, looked distantly out of the window. 'Now,' Jill said, 'whatever can this be?' She unwrapped with caution, two quilted coat-hangers. 'Oh!' she breathed. 'And another poem!'

'It's not much good,' Louisa muttered.

'I'm sure it's brilliant.

"You're Thirty-nine today,

So Happy Birthday, Mum.

You may feel rather old,

But to us you're still twenty-one!"'

Paul choked over his tea. The tray nearly upset and, helped by this distraction, Jill kissed Louisa warmly. The worst was over.

The remaining presents were from Paul. The sweater, a size bigger than last year's, would be quite possible if she took the collar off and had it dyed. She said it was lovely, and the perfume was lovely and the Braque print – she nervously turned it the right way up – was really lovely.

'I think it's perfectly ghastly,' Louisa said.

'Oh well,' Jill was amazed to hear herself saying, 'we can't all have the same tastes, can we? And it's *awfully* cheerful.' She kissed her husband gratefully. 'I don't know how to thank you,' she said. 'Such wonderful presents.'

Something was wrong, her tone of voice or what she said: there ought to be more. They waited, and she kept smiling, and at last Paul said, 'Well, you'd all better go off and get dressed or something. I'll go down and get breakfast.'

'I really don't want any,' Jill said. 'Please don't—'

'But you always have breakfast in bed on your birthday!' Louisa blazed. 'You always do!'

'Oh well, then. All right. Thank you,' she said humbly.

Left alone, she wound up all the pink ribbon which, if ironed, might still do for the party dress. She folded the wrapping paper and arranged the cards on the mantelpiece and got back into bed. A faint smell of burning crept up from the kitchen. How wonderful it is, she told herself sharply, to be loved.

The rule of her birthday was that she was not allowed to do anything. This had started when Louisa was about four. It had impressed Louisa, if no one else, as a wonderful idea and she had never allowed it to be forgotten. She was a highly organised child, very good at giving orders. Combined with remarkable beauty this made her, at twelve, rather formidable.

Unhappily dressed in the new sweater, Jill sidled downstairs at about ten o'clock. Louisa was vacuuming the sitting room.

'Why didn't you stay in bed?' she asked. 'And rest?'

'Oh well . . .' Jill said.

'It's a pity, because if it was a nice day you could sit in the garden.'

'Yes,' Jill said.

'Well, do you mind moving, because I want to Hoover over there?'

Jill went back to the bedroom and did her nails. When they were dry she thought of tidying her drawers and this reminded her that she had, for weeks, been meaning to move the chest of drawers over to the other side of the room where it would not only look better but hide a small patch of damp on the wall. She resolutely put this idea out of her head and went downstairs again. Louisa was dusting, Becky finishing the washing up. They both seemed disappointed to see her so she went and stood in the dining room for a little while, looking with interest at the rain, until Jane burst in and said, 'Oh. *You're* here. We're going to lay the table now.'

'But it's not nearly lunch time!'

'Well, that's what Louisa told me to do. Couldn't you,' she suggested sympathetically, 'go for a walk or something?'

Jill went upstairs again and looked at the chest of drawers. She closed the door and cautiously pulled out the drawers, balancing them on the bed. Then she pulled the heavy chest carefully, inch by inch, across the room. One of its feet got caught in the carpet, so she lay down on her stomach, lifting up the chest with one hand while niftily tucking the carpet down under its foot with the other. She was lying half under the bed and had just got the carpet straightened out when Louisa came in.

'I brought you some coffee,' Louisa said, and then, 'Oh! What are you *doing?*'

Jill got up and took the cup without looking at her. 'Thank you,' she said. 'I was just moving the chest of drawers.'

'But why?' Louisa wailed. 'On your birthday?'

'Oh, don't be so silly,' Jill snapped. 'Why shouldn't I move the chest of drawers on my birthday if I want to?'

'But you're meant to be resting?'

'But I don't *want* to rest!'

They glared at each other and slowly, painfully, Louisa's eyes filled with tears. Jill held out her hands, but the child turned her head away and ran down the stairs. Nobody, Jill remembered hopelessly, cried on her birthday. She knelt down and heaved savagely at the chest, upsetting the cup of coffee which poured, a scalding christening, over her new sweater.

'Louisa's thoroughly upset,' Paul said from the doorway. 'I do think you might – What on *earth* are you doing?'

'I'm trying,' she said, getting up slowly, 'to move the chest of drawers. It isn't a crime. It isn't hurting anybody. It isn't spoiling anyone's fun.'

'Look at that sweater.'

'I know.'

'It's ruined. When I think what it cost—'

'Don't tell me,' she said. 'I can always have it dyed.'

'Why can't you rise to the occasion a bit? You've thoroughly upset Louisa.'

'Is it Louisa's birthday,' she snapped suddenly, 'or mine?'

'Everyone's trying their damnedest to please you.'

'Oh, really. If that's your attitude.'

'Good God, if you can't appreciate it, I'm sorry.'

'Oh . . .' She hung her head, watching the pale grey coffee dripping on to the carpet. 'Of course I appreciate it, Paul.'

'Well, then. Now where do you want this chest of drawers?'

'Over there,' she said humbly.

He picked it up, carried it across the room and dumped it against the wall.

'Now,' he said, 'why don't you go downstairs and look at a magazine or something?'

'All right.' It struck her that they were behaving in the most curious way. He looked shifty and sick and it suddenly occurred to her that he really hated her birthday, hated her growing older. That, in fact, he was ashamed. She was certain of it. He was ashamed because he could no longer avoid knowing that she was middle aged.

'Paul—' she began.

'Well?' He had his back to her, pushing in the drawers.

She couldn't think what to say. 'Do you love me?'

'Of course. You might just have a word with Louisa. She tries hard on your birthday.'

'I know,' she said. 'You all do.'

'Well, then. I'll go and get the lunch. You just relax. You know – relax a bit.'

'Yes,' she said. 'All right.'

He went heavily downstairs. She sat down on the bed and began pulling the fluff off the blanket, rolling it between her finger and thumb.

• • •

The play, this year, concerned two princes captured by a wicked wizard and saved in the nick of time by a benevolent fairy aged thirty-nine. Last year it had been two princesses captured by a wicked witch and saved in the nick of time by a benevolent fairy aged thirty-eight. Jane and Becky played the princes and Louisa doubled for the other parts. It was full of 'Oho!' and 'By my troth!' and 'Whither away?' After each scene Jane applauded loudly and was scolded by Louisa. In the interval, while Louisa was bringing up the birthday cake and ice cream, Jane and Becky danced to a long-playing record of Sidney Bechet. As time wore on their faces became grimmer and their breathing louder, but they continued to lollop bravely about and never moved their eyes from the audience, which kept smiles of appreciation clamped firmly on both their faces. At last the record ended, Jill cut the cake and remembered to wish.

'What did you wish?' Jane asked.

'Don't be silly. She can't tell. Come on, we've got to do the second scene now.'

They hurried busily away.

'It's a lovely play,' Jill said timidly. 'Are you all right?'

Her husband nodded. He was absolutely exhausted and had put down four dry martinis before lunch in order to nerve himself for the washing up. Jill had changed into a dress and made up her face with great care. In spite of this, she had begun to feel slightly hysterical. It was not surely necessary for the fairy to grow so old?

'Gadzooks!' Louisa cried, looking evil, 'those princes will make me a jolly fine supper . . .'

At the end of the play the entire cast sang God Save The Queen and Happy Birthday To You. Then the curtains were drawn back and Jane inexplicably burst into tears. Becky, too, hung about looking moistly through her enormous glasses.

'They're tired,' Jill muttered, patting them hopelessly, 'I'll put them to bed.'

'You can't,' Louisa said, looking disgusted under her benevolent fairy's crown. 'It's your birthday. You're going out. I'll put them, if they're such babies.'

'But I'm sure there's time—'

'You wouldn't want Mummy to bath you, would you? On her birthday?'

Dumb, guilty, swamped in tears, Jane shook her head.

'Then come on.' A tinsel and muslin wardress, she pushed them out of the room. 'And if you're good,' Jill heard her saying, 'you can watch television for half an hour but, mind you, not a minute longer.' Their voices, like the voices of tired, nattering old women, retreated up the stairs.

Jill tidied the sitting room and poured herself a drink. The day weighed heavily on her, like some expensive mistake, a lapse of good taste which, once paid for, is irrevocable. The bonfire had been extinguished by the day's rain. Some of the leaves on the laburnum had turned yellow overnight, but this was the only sign of autumn. The air had become clear and watery as spring and birds were twittering and fussing in the tall, grimy trees. The year, yesterday so mellow, had become petrified in a grey, damp evening.

'Well, shall we go?'

She turned reluctantly. Paul had changed his suit, but not his expression. He went straight over to the decanter and poured himself a triple whisky.

'Yes,' she said. 'When you're ready.'

'I'm ready now.'

'All right, then. Let's go.'

'Well, what do you mean, when I'm ready.'

'Nothing. Where are we going?'

'Where do we always go on your birthday? Pierre's, of course.'

'How silly of me,' she said. 'I should have known.'

They came home, rather unsteadily and in silence, about eleven. The children were all asleep. The house felt surprisingly normal, freed from tension. There was even a banana skin in the sitting-room grate which Louisa hadn't tidied away. They climbed slowly upstairs, not speaking, yawned and sighed in the cold bedroom. It's over, they both thought, pulling off their shoes. Weariness, apathy, drowned them. They moved about the room as languidly and pointlessly as fish in a small tank. When, at last, she had turned down the coverlet, put his pyjamas ready on the pillow, opened the window, turned off the main light, he was still standing in his shirt looking vaguely about the room. She had already forgotten about her birthday. Her face, after an enormous yawn, settled back lax and unsmiling.

'Do hurry,' she said. 'I'm dropping.'

He picked up his pyjamas, looked at them with distaste and let them fall in a heap on the floor. Then he wandered to the cupboard, took out a clean pair of pyjamas and began, with laborious concentration, to undo the buttons.

In one movement she sat upright. Her whole body was stiff and trembling. 'You can't,' she said, 'wear clean pyjamas.'

He lowered towards her, his head stuck forward. 'Why not?'

'You had clean pyjamas last night.'

'And is there any reason,' he enquired, skidding a little over the words, 'why I shouldn't have clean pyjamas tonight as well?'

'Of course there is!' She was desolate, outraged. 'We can't afford the laundry! You said so yourself! We can't afford the laundry!'

At last he let fly. 'Then why don't you wash them yourself instead of fooling around all day moving the furniture?'

'Why should I wash your horrible pyjamas? Why should I?'

'Don't shout,' he said. 'I cannot stand you shouting.'

'Why shouldn't I shout?'

'Because,' he said, 'you are too old.'

They stared at each other. All sound, even the sound of breathing, had stopped. He went out of the room, carrying the clean pyjamas. He went downstairs. She heard the sitting room door close.

He had drunk too much, of course. It had been a strain. She had only been trying to save him the expense of the laundry. He was overtired. He would soon come back and apologise. She turned off the bedside light and lay on her back, staring at the patterns of the street lamp on the ceiling. The clock chimed and began to strike midnight. Next year, she realised, I shall be forty. She lay waiting, the little smile of gratitude fixed on her face, a distant welcome.

DAUNT BOOKS

Founded in 2010, the Daunt Books imprint
is dedicated to discovering brilliant works
by talented authors from around the world.
Whether reissuing beautiful new editions
of lost classics or introducing fresh literary
voices, we're drawn to writing that evokes a
strong sense of place – novels, short fiction,
memoirs, travel accounts, and translations
with a lingering atmosphere, a thrilling story,
and a distinctive style. With our roots as a
travel bookshop, the titles we publish are
inspired by the Daunt shops themselves, and
the exciting atmosphere of discovery to be
found in a good bookshop.

For more information, please visit
www.dauntbookspublishing.co.uk